BODY
HEART
SOUL

BLIND VOWS
VOLUME 2

BY: J.M. WITT

ACKNOWLEDGMENTS

Thank you to everyone who's read my work and continues to do so.

Darren Birks: Thank you for being such a pleasure to work with. You've been nothing but supportive and your willingness to help has gone above and beyond. Thank you. You'll always be my Heathcliff and FitzWilliam!

Dione: You're gorgeous. Thank you for proving that beauty doesn't discriminate. Thank you for being my Des!

Rebecca, Betsy, and Leticia: WOW. You three were bombarded with this secret project and took off running with me. Thank you for your overwhelming support and belief in me. Words will never be enough to express what it means to me.

Tami, Tracey, and Elaine: Three more of the most supportive fans and friends a girl could ask for. Thank you!

Stacey and Jaime: Well, what else is there to say, but 'Give the man some head!'

Tyf and Skye: There are no words for me to say. Your friendship means the world to me. I never would've made it this far without you two. I love you dearly.

Bloggers: Thank you, thank you, thank you.

To my friends and family: Thank you for your support. You know who you are!

TABLE OF CONTENTS

TABLE OF CONTENTS CONT.

Soul

BODY

~ DESIREE ~

~ CHAPTER 1 ~

I stepped out of the bathroom after changing out of my work clothes. The girls teased me and joked about the outfit I wore, especially given the cold temps outside. It's true, I was on the prowl. I wore heels, a miniskirt, and a flowy top that showed more cleavage than necessary. I was headed out to get laid, not looking for a soulmate. Being a doctor had its own issues. In this outfit, nothing about it said I was a doctor, therefore, I couldn't intimidate someone insecure and wasn't likely to attract someone after a sugar momma. Looking to my hands, I realized I'd left my bag with my work clothes in the bathroom. When I re-emerged from the bathroom, head down, I ran smack into someone.

"Oh, God. I'm sorry." He managed to keep his balance, and I noticed immediately the prosthetic leg from the way he moved. He was a patient. "Are you alright?"

As he shifted his weight with one hand on my shoulder, he reluctantly removed it. He made eye contact with me, which impressed me. Most men couldn't do that, not with what I was wearing and that was the point. His hazel eyes had a permanent sadness about them and I knew he was trouble, I just wasn't sure what kind. He'd been coming here for therapy for quite some time, though he wasn't my patient. I'd filled in for another therapist a week earlier and worked with him. I couldn't work with him again.

I walked into my session that day, with a patient I hadn't worked with before. His normal therapist had called in sick. Looking over his chart, I grew familiar with his history. Left leg amputation just over a year ago during service. I wasn't sure what to expect when I walked in and he far exceeded any expectation I had.

"Odysseus Kerrigan?"

"That's me."

I lifted my head and felt like the wind had been knocked from my lungs. He was something else. Then he smiled. Dropping my eyes, I cleared my throat, "Can I call you Odysseus?"

Grinning, "You can call me anything you want." I stared back at him dumbfounded as he apologized. "Sorry, you can call me O."

He stretched out his hand and I warily placed my hand in his. A spark I hadn't felt—well I wasn't sure how long it'd been—ran up my arm and down my back. I reminded myself that I had a set of rules to follow. Never get involved with patients...EVER AGAIN!

"Are you alright?"

"I'm good. You?" I just nodded my head in response when he asked, "I thought I'd be seeing you today for my session?"

"What?" I was at a loss for words, momentarily forgetting that I'd switched my schedule, not wanting to see him. I mean, I wanted to see him, but I couldn't go there. *Get a grip Des!* "Yes. Sorry, there was a scheduling conflict.

"So you're not avoiding me?"

"There's nothing to avoid, Mr. Kerrigan. You're a patient and that's all it can ever be."

"So, if I'm not *your* patient then we can be more?"

I wasn't sure if he was asking a question or making a statement. The hopeless romantic I'd been as a teenager jumped up and down in my head chanting, 'Be more, be more!' "For the love…"

I must've spoken out loud because he inquired, "For the love… You want more or you want me as your patient? Which is it? Both, maybe?"

I couldn't help but smile at his brazenness. "I don't think either is a good idea."

He pursed his lips and then asked me more questions. He wasn't going to give up easily. "Why? You're a great therapist. Do I smell? You already said you're single." Something I'd unintentionally let slip out the prior week. "Are you not attracted to me? Maybe you're a lesbian?"

I started laughing and let my mouth talk before I thought about what I was going to say, "I'm not a lesbian, O. I'm attracted to you and that's the problem."

His eyes twinkled and his bright white teeth shone as his face broke into a smile. "Feeling's mutual." I stood there in horror realizing what I'd just confessed to him, but I was also a little shook up. He was attracted to me, too. "So, we just need to clear up this name thing of yours and I'll be able to officially ask you out. Let's do this again, pretend we just met."

"What are you talking about?" I was completely frazzled. His lips were moving, he was talking, but my brain was still processing the knowledge that he was attracted to me. I was old! He was young, maybe too young.

He stuck his hand out, introducing himself, "I'm O. And who might you be?"

Ok. He wanted to play this game, I'd gladly play. "O? Your name's O?" I gave him my hand and there it was again. He didn't release my hand, just kept talking.

One corner of his mouth turned up as he confirmed, "It's Odysseus, but everyone calls me O."

"Odysseus? Seriously? I thought I hated my name."

His eyes narrowed, knowing I was playing with him, as he clarified, "I didn't say I hated my name."

"Right, sorry. Bad assumption."

"So, what's so horrible about *your* name…?"

He was still waiting for me to answer him when one of the receptionists walked by. I pried my hand from his before she saw. "Have a good weekend, Des!" I'd made certain years ago that everyone call me Des, not Dr. Greene.

"Des. Let me guess." He rubbed his fingers on his chin and the five o'clock shadow lurking there. "Destiny?" I shook my head. "Desdemona?"

Giggling, I said, "No. Keep trying."

"Hmm. I'm not up to date with female D names, but I have two brothers with them and I can't imagine it's one of their names."

He'd peaked my curiosity, "What are their names?"

"You wouldn't believe me if I told you."

"Try me."

"Dorian and D'Artagnan."

I held in a chuckle as I said, "Dorian isn't bad, but D'Artagnan? Your mom a fan of literature or something?"

"Or something. She's actually a literature professor."

Slowly, I nodded my head while thinking his mom must be a complete cuckoo, "Explains a lot. I can only imagine the names your sisters got stuck with."

Smiling, "Nope, all boys. There are five of us."

"Five! No thank you." I wanted kids, at least I thought I did, but my time was running out. It was then that I remembered I was almost ten years older than him, though he'd never guess that.

"Nah, it was nice. We're all close in age. It has its perks."

My cell began to ring and when I pulled it out I realized I was late. How long had I stood there talking to O, completely forgetting my plans? Flashing my phone, I said, "I should get this. Nice chatting with you." He just stood there as I answered the phone. "Hang on." I put the phone against my chest as O began speaking again.

"Des, what do I need to do?" I tilted my head, not sure how to respond. "I promise I'm not crazy."

The last guy who turned out to be crazy had promised he wasn't crazy either. "O, it's not you. It's me."

"Really? You're feeding me that line?" He took a step closer and my heart rate picked up. "I think you're perfect." He gently pulled a tendril of my hair through his fingers as he said, "Think about it."

Think about what? Before I could actually form the words to ask him, he nodded and began walking away and I won't deny that I watched him do so. Lifting the phone back to my ear, I told my cousin, Stacey, I'd be there soon. It'd been too long since we'd seen one another and she was on the prowl as well. We were meeting for dinner and then from there who knew what the night held.

After putting on my winter coat, I walked to the parking lot and spotted him climbing into his truck, or maybe he spotted me. "You never told me your full name." I stopped in my tracks and put my hands on my hips.

Walking over to him, he closed the door and rolled down the window. "Do you have a piece of paper?" It was against my better judgement, but there was something about him...

Handing me his phone, he said, "All I have is this."

I took it from him and programmed my name *Des* and my phone number in it before quickly texting myself so I'd have his number as well. "Here you go."

He looked at the screen and called after me, "What's Des short for?"

"Wait and you may find out!" I climbed into my Challenger and drove off, well aware of him staring after me. Pulling up my text to talk, I sent him a message.

> *If you want to know,*
> *meet me at O'Grady's.*

Stacey and I enjoyed our dinner, but O never showed up. Just another reason why I didn't involve myself with patients. Now I just had to hope I didn't run into him at work. Rejection wasn't something I handled well and it wasn't something I was used to, especially with how persistent he'd been today. Stacey had left the bar with a 'friend' and I stayed behind hoping to find a 'friend' of my own.

The next morning I rolled over 'Coyote Ugly' style. I didn't even remember his name, only remembered that he was a distraction. I'd followed him to his place where we'd cut right to the chase. Ripped condom packets littered the floor and the ache between my legs was the only other confirmation I needed that I'd accomplished my mission.

Get laid.

Check.

Now it was time to go.

Slipping my clothes back on and with my shoes in my hand, I grabbed my purse and slipped out the door. Once I sat down in my car, I exhaled, finally able to breathe again. Turning the engine, I dropped my head back and recalled my convo with O the previous afternoon. I made a mental note to find out when his next appointment was so that we would cross paths very little, if at all, at work.

Then I got angry. Why did I give a fuck? He clearly wasn't interested or he would've shown up at O'Grady's. I thought I had spotted him after leaving the restroom, but after fighting through the bar crowd, I couldn't find him anywhere. Wishful thinking on my part. Then I wondered if something had happened to him. *Stop it!* I'd gotten the wrong idea when he was pursuing me. It was probably just a game to him. Guys his age were just about the chase. That's it. *Drowning* by Banks was playing and I turned it up as I calmed my nerves. Hell, maybe he was married. And flirting with me. *Pig!*

~ DESIREE ~

~ CHAPTER 2 ~

A few weeks passed and I'd seen O on the schedule and kept clear of him. He wasn't my patient and I made sure I was busy with my own, or took a late lunch to avoid seeing him. No one seemed to be the wiser and I was fine with it that way.

Thursday of that week I walked into my session and was blindsided. There he stood. He wasn't on my schedule and I looked at the file I held which clearly wasn't O's file. He smiled at me as if no wrongs had ever been done and it was the straw that broke my back.

I stormed out of the room and marched to the front desk. "You pulled the wrong file. I need Odysseus Kerrigan's file." The girls were taken aback by my tone and immediately scrambled to find O's file. Growing impatient, I snapped, "Bring me the file when you find it."

Marching back into the room, I found him pacing the floor. He walked over and asked, "Is everything alright?"

Closing my eyes, I took a deep breath and then said, "No, it's not. They pulled the wrong file and you're not supposed to be on my rotation."

"So are you mad that I'm here or mad about the file?"

"God dammit, O!"

The door opened and the file was dropped on the counter without a word. Walking over, I flipped open the file. My eyes couldn't even focus on the log sheets. I hung my head and pressed my temples, trying to relieve the pressure that had suddenly built up.

A hand came down on my shoulder sending an instant calm over me. "Des?" At the sound of my name falling from his lips, I relaxed as he pulled me closer, the warmth of his chest seeping into my back. "I came to O'Grady's that night."

Lies! Realizing that I was in an almost precarious situation with a patient, I leapt away from him, spitting out, "No. You don't get to do this."

"Do what? Pursue a mutual attraction?"

"No, yes. We can't pursue this." I stormed out of the room and told the front desk to reschedule him ASAP, but not with me, stating there was a conflict of interest. I scuttled to my office and locked the door before I collapsed in my chair.

What was this pull he had over me? I was a fucking grown woman and he had me acting like a giddy teenager. A boy liked me, he really liked me—or so he said. But, like boys do, he played me. Now if I could just get my body to stop reacting to him I could possibly try to move on, like there was anything to move on from.

I stepped out of my office long after his appointment should've ended and made my way to my car. I wasn't even paying attention to my surroundings when I opened the car door. Sliding in the driver's seat, I saw a note under my wiper. Sighing, I climbed out and grabbed it assuming it was some solicitor's advertisement.

When I read it I knew immediately who it was from. My skin crawled and my stomach flipped. Like a reflex I locked my car doors right as a tap came to my window. I screamed and looked, seeing O. Putting his hands up, he took a step back. I took a deep breath and rolled down the window.

"Sorry. I didn't mean to scare you."

Relief flooded me at the sight of O as I shook my head and glanced in my side mirrors and rearview mirrors before looking back to O. "You didn't." I crumpled the note and threw it to the passenger side floor.

He didn't miss a beat. Eyeing the note and then me, he asked, "That's what scared you?"

Pressing my lips together in a tight smile, I lied. "It's nothing. Just an admirer."

"An *admirer* or a *stalker*?"

"Really, it's nothing to worry about." That was bullshit and I knew it and apparently O knew it, too. I had a PPO out against *him* and knew I should report the note to the cops.

"You're scared."

I wasn't sure what it was, but I trusted O. I didn't want to, but I did. There was no fighting it. I wanted and needed to trust someone and although my heart often misled my head, both told me I could trust him. "You're right."

"About?"

I must've been out of my mind. "Can you follow me to the police station? I need to report this."

He nodded and agreed, "Absolutely. Would you rather I drive you?" He saw the look on my face and added, "Or I can ride with you."

"Sorry. Um, can you just follow me?"

"Yup. You got it."

We got to the station a few minutes later. O walked in with me and I went to the desk asking to speak to an officer. O waited with me in the lobby until an officer came to get me.

"Desiree Greene?" I stood and shook the officer's hand and he motioned me to sit back down. "What's going on? I see that you have an active PPO out on Sa..."

I stopped him short, never wanting to hear his name again. "Yes, please don't say his name." Pulling the note from my purse, I handed it to the officer. "I found it on my windshield after work."

"Any clue what time it was put there? Did you go out to lunch?"

"I didn't see it there before my appointment, but it was there when I left."

The officer looked over at O and asked, "And who might you be?"

"He's a patient, Odysseus Kerrigan."

"And how do I know *he* didn't place the note on your windshield?"

I shook my head persistently, annoyance dripping off my tongue. "It was *him*. I know how he works. He disappears just long enough for me to think he's finally gone. O has nothing to do with this."

The detective nodded and held open a baggy as I placed the note inside, knowing my fingerprints had probably contaminated it. "We'll add it to the file and pay him a visit." He stood and we did the same. "You have someone who can stay with you tonight or somewhere you can go?" He glanced to O as I objected.

"That's not necessary."

"I can stay with her."

I smiled and tried to remain calm. I wasn't helpless and didn't need O's protection. I had a gun, a permit, and I knew how to use it. We walked out of the police station as I announced to him, "You're NOT staying with me. I can take care of myself."

"I'm sure you can, but you have a PPO out on this guy—whoever he is—for a reason. You're not staying alone. You won't win this one. Besides, Officer what's-his-name is expecting it."

Glaring at him, I rolled my eyes. "Don't get any ideas. I have a gun and I'm not afraid to use it."

"That's good to know Des, or should I call you Desiree?"

"Ugh! Des, call me Des. I hate that name."

"I think it's beautiful. Gets me thinking all kinds of things." He glanced at me, he was testing me; I knew it.

Sarcastically, I egged him on, "What kind of things? Hmm? Ideas about desire with Desiree? Like I haven't heard that before."

Grinning he corrected, "No, I was thinking more about you showing me your O face." I smacked him as he laughed, "Got you to smile."

"I did not!"

"You did! I understand." He was charming, I'd give him that. "The thought of me naked in bed should put a smile on your face."

"You're ridiculous!" Of course now all I was thinking about was seeing *his* O face. I unlocked my car and climbed in. "Maybe you can show me your O face later, if you can keep up. I'm hungry. You know where I'll be." I prayed I wasn't setting myself up for disappointment once again. O was a risky bet but I felt like it was a good one that would play in my favor.

He looked slightly baffled before he understood. I pulled out of the parking lot as he backed out of his spot. I was headed to O'Grady's and if he had a clue, he'd figure that out. I parked behind the bar a few minutes later and started walking through the parking lot. A horn honked and I jumped in the air in response.

His truck pulled up next to me as he shouted at me, "You know, frequenting the same joints probably isn't the smartest thing considering you have a stalker. Just a thought."

"Let me guess. You worked Military Intelligence?" He didn't say anything and I just shook it off and walked into the bar without him.

The bar was packed so I opted for a booth. The hostess was leading me back and once I sat down, O appeared behind her and glared at me. He took his seat, his prosthetic kicking me as he apologized.

"It's ok. Would a table be better?"

"No. It's fine. I just need to get situated."

I looked over the menu, not entirely sure why because I always ordered the same thing. Setting the menu down, I glanced at him as he looked over his own menu. The waitress came and we placed our orders. Then the awkward silence began. I didn't know what to say or where to start. Thank God he broke the quiet.

"So, Des. Tell me about yourself."

"Not much to tell."

Taking a sip of my water, he stared at me over the rim of my glass. Setting it down, I questioned, "What?"

"You're full of shit."

"Excuse me? I didn't stand *you* up. That was you!"

"Ouch! So that's what this is about? This attitude of yours?"

"I don't have an attitude."

"Yes, you do." He put his hand up to stop me from interrupting him. "It's not what you think. By the time I had the nerve to show up, you were already cozied up with someone else."

Coyote Ugly. "I..." Was it possible that seeing him in the crowd that night hadn't been a figment of my imagination?

"Nope, you don't need to explain. We're grown adults. But, I'm not into playing games either."

I didn't even know what to say. Without saying it, he'd made me feel cheap and easy. Maybe he was right. I tried to remember how long I actually waited for him that night and couldn't recall. It probably wasn't long. I deserved his ire.

He took a deep breath and whispered, "I'm sorry. You're upset. That wasn't my intention."

"Could've fooled me."

"Damn. Who was he? Who fucked you so hard over a barrel that you're so cold and shut off?"

"Excuse me? Who do you think you are?" I got up to leave and his hand came down over mine. I wanted to pull my hand away, but was enjoying the sensations running up my arm as his thumb caressed the top my hand.

"Des, please. You may not believe me, but I like you, a lot. I can't get you out of my head. Where's the girl I met at PT? She was cool, no walls, just a girl getting to know a boy. Then you remembered that I was a patient with a mutual attraction and the walls came flying back up." I stared at him, sure the confusion was written all over my face. "You're the first person since it happened not to look at me with pity in your eyes. That means a lot to me."

I knew what he was referring to. I'd gotten familiar with his chart. *It* had happened just over a year ago and he'd been fitted with the prosthetic about six months later. He'd made quicker progress than most and it spoke volumes about his character and determination. In fact, he probably didn't need to be coming to weekly PT sessions anymore and that piqued my interest.

"You've been released from PT. Why do you still come?"

Blinking once, his hazel eyes stared into mine as he revealed, "Why do you think?" Fear and trepidation would have been my normal reaction had someone else said that to me. But with O, warmth spread through me in response to his statement.

The waitress placed our food down and I immediately started eating. He was too young for me. I had eight years on him. All the reasons why it couldn't work out ran rampant through my head. I had money, but not like you'd think, so he'd be disappointed if he thought I was loaded. I'd completed med school, barely, to then pursue physical therapy instead. So while I really was a doctor, a true MD would consider me a quitter even though I had the student loans to prove it. The only extravagant thing in my life was my car, the one thing I let myself indulge in.

"You're overthinking. What is it?"

"Christ. You telepathic or something?"

"I'm just good at reading people. Always have been."

I set my burger down and finished chewing. "I'm too old for you."

He just surveyed my face and then countered, "No you're not. How old do you think I am?" I looked away and he laughed. "Right. You know exactly how old I am. You're not too old."

"We're not talking a couple years O. I have almost a decade on you."

He didn't even flinch. "Lucky you. I get you in your prime and you get a young stallion." Then he winked.

I just shook my head, smiling. "You're ridiculous."

"That's what you like about me." He studied my eyes for a moment before confessing, "I'm not asking for forever. But I am asking for more than one or two nights and maybe a few dates with a chance of forever." He munched on a fry and then said, "You can pick your chin up off the floor." Snapping my mouth shut I returned my eyes to my food. "What are you so afraid of?"

Looking at him, I took in his face. Strong cheekbones, tousled brown hair that the sun had lightened slightly, a kissable chin, and those sad hazel eyes that currently shone green. He was beautiful, yet rugged with his five o'clock shadow.

I *was* afraid. Afraid of the way my heart raced with him near, afraid of the way he looked at me like I was more than a potential lay, and afraid of the way I knew he'd steal my heart—denying that he probably already had. If I let him. I couldn't let that happen. I wouldn't let that happen.

"I'm not afraid."

"You're petrified."

~ DESIREE ~

~ CHAPTER 3 ~

"Ok. You need to stop that." I went to get up again and he tried to stop me. "I'll be right back." Reaching in my purse, I said, "Here. My keys. I'm not leaving." He glanced at my keys as I placed them on the table between us. He released my hand and I hurried off to the bathroom.

I looked in the mirror and whispered, "Jesus fuck. Get a grip, Des." I mentally reiterated his words. He wasn't looking for forever, *just a few dates with a possibility of forever.* Why did I suddenly want more? Forever with him didn't sound bad. What was happening? He was playing me and that didn't happen often. *I* was the player. Could it be that he wasn't playing me, just very assertive and fucking persistent? Tilting my head from side to side, I took a breath and walked back to the table.

"You alright?"

Nodding, I smiled, "Yes. You?"

His brows raised as he nodded in return. "So, how old are you that you think you're *too* old?"

"How old do you think I am?"

"Nope. I'm not playing that game. You said you had a decade on me, but I wouldn't put you a day over thirty five."

"I'll be thirty five in June."

"I'll be twenty seven in May. Only 8 years older."

"Only. If the roles were reversed..." My attention was momentarily drawn to the song playing overhead. *I Don't Wanna Grow Up* by Bebe Rexha started its whimsical beginning as her lyrics filled my ears. Ironic how she was singing about how she didn't want to grow up and I was afraid of being too grown up.

O cleared his throat, garnering my attention. "Yes, if the roles were reversed no one would say a thing. Ten years ago, when I was a teenager, it might have been frowned upon, but I'm a grown man."

"That's debatable."

Laughing, he threw his head back. "That's it, isn't it? He was younger than you."

"Who?"

"You tell me. Whoever hurt you." There were too many men who'd hurt me, but the first one always hurt the worst. He pursed his lips. "Yup, that's it. Guess I have my work cut out for me."

"His name was Mike. He was only a couple years younger and the worst mistake of my life. I spent years paying for his mistakes and my foolishness. I was in med school and he racked up so much debt, and in my name no less." Why was I telling him all of this?

"Sounds like a real winner." I narrowed my eyes at him as he smirked. "You live and learn. Sounds like he took advantage of you, and if you were in med school you had other priorities to focus on. I'd never do that." Pausing, he then asked, "Is there more?"

Shrugging my shoulders I wondered if he meant more men or more shitty things done by Mike. I decided to stick with the Mike story and added, "When I found out about the debt, around the time we got evicted—because he hadn't been paying the rent—I had entrusted him with that, too. Anyway, he started talking about having kids and getting married. I lost my shit on him. We couldn't pay rent. How the hell were we supposed to support a kid? It wasn't long before he was gone, but of course my dad had to pay him off."

"What?"

It was laughable now, but it was true. "Yup. My dad asked him how much it would take for him to walk out of my life." O just stared at me, dumbfounded. "Would you like to guess what price tag he put on my love?"

His answer stunned even me. "Love doesn't have a price tag, Des." My heart jumped up and down like an obnoxious cheerleader, chanting his name. 'O, O, O!'

"Ha, yeah, well it did to Mike. Five hundred bucks." O's eyes about bulged out of his head as I took another bite of my burger, which suddenly lost all its flavor.

"He walked away from you for five hundred dollars?" He stared at me in disbelief. "What a fucking douche nozzle."

"Love. Isn't it grand?"

"Uh, that's not love."

"Yeah, could you go back and convince me of that. I'd appreciate it." We both laughed and I pushed my plate to the edge of the table, my appetite gone. I wondered if he'd ever been in love, but also didn't have the courage to ask him. Not yet.

His hand reached for mine and the sensations that ran through me at his touch scared the crap out of me, but in a good way. "You're worth a hell of a lot more, Des."

I took a deep breath, letting him twine our fingers together, and barely got out my words. "You sure lay it on thick."

"It'd take at least twice that to get me to walk away." I let out a silent laugh and shook my head at him, knowing he was messing with me. Winking, he softly proclaimed, "In all seriousness, it's the truth. You're worth a hell of a lot more. I'm not a bull-shitter. Maybe a little too assertive for some, but that's about it."

I believed him. The check came and he released my hand, snatching up the check before I could. I didn't try to fight him for it, knowing it was pointless.

He followed me to my apartment, though I still thought it was unnecessary. Taking the elevator up to my floor, I opened the door and he immediately scoped the place out before letting me in.

"You should get cameras. There are a lot of potential security risks. An alarm would be wise, too, maybe some more deadbolts."

Rolling my eyes, I acquiesced. "Yes, sir."

"I'm serious, Des. You're vulnerable here."

"I have a gun. I can take care of myself."

He proceeded to check all my windows before he seemed satisfied. I left him sitting on the couch and went to my bedroom to change out of my work clothes. I emerged in yoga pants and a t-shirt, my feet bare.

"You don't have to stay."

"I'm not going anywhere."

I chewed the inside of my lower lip. I was out of my element with a man in my apartment for the purpose of protecting me. I didn't have men in my apartment. It was another unwritten rule of mine. "Um, can I get you something to drink?"

"Water's fine."

Before sitting down on the other end of the couch, I handed him a glass of water while sipping on my own. "So what now?"

I swore the corner of his mouth turned up in a smile and his eyes sparkled. "Don't worry, Des. I won't be having my way with you. Not tonight."

"Scared?" He started coughing, not expecting my response. Leaning in, I patted his back as he got his breathing back under control. "Sorry. I tend to give as good as I get."

"I'm getting that. Don't stop on my account. It's refreshing. Reminds me of someone I know."

Tilting my head, I inquired, "Who might that be?"

"No worries. She's just a friend, my sister-in-law actually, Lucy. You'd like her. She and my brother are constantly bantering with one another. It's fun to watch."

Her name sounded familiar. There couldn't be that many Lucy's around, but I didn't question it. "Sounds like they're fun." He just nodded. "What is it?"

"Nothing. I envy what they have." He caught my expression and became defensive. "No, no! I'm not lusting after her. She's like a sister, literally. They both fought their feelings for each other for so long and now, well, now the devil himself couldn't tear them apart. They were great people apart, but with their forces combined..."

"Yes?"

"They just opened a gym up north and it's doing really well. They're a great team."

"It's a rare thing. You can love someone, but to be able to work with them all day, too." I blew out a sharp breath, "I don't think I could work alongside my spouse. People need their space."

"Maybe you haven't found the right person?"

"Maybe."

I'd watched my mother lose herself in my father. So much so that she had no life of her own, no friends of her own. Her life was his. When I was old enough to recognize that, I swore my life would be different. I wouldn't be dependent on my spouse to fill my days. Don't get me wrong. My mom was a great wife and mom, but *that* was her identity and I promised myself more.

I covered my mouth as a yawn took over. "You don't have to stay up on my account."

Shaking my head, I refused. "No. It's not even that late and it's the weekend."

"It's after ten."

"It is?" I looked at the clock and it confirmed what he said. "Shit. I can put a movie in."

"Your call."

I got up and picked the first movie that caught my attention. It was one I loved, but hadn't watched in a long time. Sitting back down, I hit play and waited for the menu to load. He'd commandeered the good spot on the couch and I debated about moving closer or just dealing with it.

"Do you want to switch spots?"

"No, it's ok. You're the guest."

"You can come closer." My eyes searched his and he put his hands up in defense. "I'll behave. Scout's honor."

"Boy scout, huh?" He nodded. "Then surely I'm safe." I moved down next to him, my leg barely grazing his, and tried ignoring what his closeness did to my heart rate. His arm moved behind me and I looked at him, "Don't try anything Mr. Kerrigan."

"Just getting comfortable." He winked as the main menu popped up on the TV. "Willow?"

"Have you seen it?"

"Are you kidding? With three older brothers, it was unavoidable. 'Out of the way peck!'" We both laughed before he added, "Will had a mad crush on the female. What was her name?"

"Sorsha."

"Yes. He's a sucker for redheads."

"Aren't all men?"

"Meh. I'm not picky."

"That's good."

I hit play and it wasn't long before my back was leaning comfortably into his side. I'd catch myself staring at his hand that sat perfectly content on the back of the couch. Did I want him to touch me? Of course, but I knew the danger that could come from it, too.

~ DESIREE ~

~ CHAPTER 4 ~

I don't remember falling asleep, but when I woke I found myself in his lap. Something else was happening and I kept my eyes closed as I figured out what the wonderful sensation was. He was stroking my hair. His fingers gently pulled through my long strands making it hard for me to open my eyes. There was a pillow under my head and I could feel the expansion of his chest as he breathed, the slight movement gently rocking me.

Forcing my eyes open, I wasn't sure what I'd find. His eyes were focused on mine by the time I adjusted to the darkness. He continued combing my hair with his fingers as I stretched and apologized.

"Sorry. I didn't mean to fall asleep."

"It's ok. I didn't mind. You didn't last long."

"I'm old and lame. Told you that already."

"You're not old. Maybe a little lame." He mocked as my brows furrowed at him. "Relax, Des."

His fingers pulled on the delicate strands at the nape of my neck as I tried to suppress the chill that ran over me. I didn't know what to do or say, lost for words. His free hand came off the back of the couch and stroked my face. My eyes closed in response. The soft pad of his finger ran over my eyebrow and down my cheek. I opened my eyes just as his thumb ran over my slightly parted lips and my breathing hitched.

Pressing my lips together I stared at his face. He seemed almost lost in thought. He was looking at me, but it was like he saw right through me. "O?"

His eyes focused on mine again and he pulled his hand away from my mouth. "I'm sorry. I promised I wouldn't touch you."

"I don't mind." *Danger, danger, Des.* Get it together. My hand found his wrist and guided his hand back to my face. "Do it again. Please."

His breathing increased as he resumed touching my face. "Des. You're so beautiful. Do you even have any idea?" His knees shifted, lifting me higher and his face lowered to hover above mine. "Tell me stop now, Des."

I didn't tell him anything. Instead my hands moved to his face, cupping his stubble covered cheeks as I pulled his mouth closer to mine. "I never promised to keep my hands to myself."

A small moan escaped him as his eyes closed and half a second later his warm full lips were on mine. Closing my eyes, I inhaled deeply as my stomach flipped and my heart raced. I hadn't had this reaction to a man's touch in too long. So long that I'd lost hope of ever feeling it again.

O smelled good, no, great. He smelled like sanctuary and I wanted him closer. My fingers moved to the nape of his neck and threaded through his overgrown locks. He was being a gentleman, taking the kiss slow with no tongue. Just his lips nipping at mine and I couldn't control myself any longer. I waited for the right moment and licked his upper lip just as it settled between mine. Groaning, he stilled as I took over the kiss. Licking and sucking on his lips as his hands began to roam my body. Finally, his tongue met mine and the sound that left my throat startled me.

Smiling against my lips, he whispered, "Want me to stop?"

"Don't you dare!"

His kiss grew deeper and my body convulsed as his hand ran across my bare belly. My shirt hem now pooled under my heaving breasts as his fingers moved over my abdomen. Christ. If I didn't get myself under control I was going to come before we got to the good part. His mouth left mine and moved to my neck. Lifting my chin to give him better access, his hand moved to my hip and his fingers moved under the material, fingering the band of my tanga panties. Just as quickly he pulled his hand away and moved it over my clothed thigh. I groaned in disapproval, but I wasn't sure he knew that.

I was completely transfixed in the moment and felt young again, younger than I had in a very long time. My blood was pumping everywhere causing my clit to throb, my nipples to pucker, and my stomach to twirl. The need to feel more was all consuming as I relaxed in his lap. His hand was at my knee and slowly moving higher. He avoided the place I needed his touch most, my hips arched, seeking his touch.

"Christ, you're sexy." His lips came back down on mine before I could respond. "Tell me what you want, Des." His breath filled my mouth with his plea.

Panting, I begged, "Please touch me, O." My eyes opened to meet his as he pulled his face back. I found his hand resting on my hip and I guided it just above my mound. "Here."

He took a shaky breath, asking, "You're sure?" Nodding, I pushed his hand a little lower and he smirked at me, regaining control of his hand. "Patience grasshopper."

Kissing me slowly and deeply, my brain became a pile of mush as my body seemed to fall off its axis of sanity. I no longer knew which way was up and which was down. His hand moved under my shirt and cupped my breast through the lacy material of my bra. I lifted slightly, pulling the shirt from my body as his eyes examined my chest. Gently, he pulled the cup down as my breast popped free. The warmth of his palm covering me had me moaning as I lifted my breast higher, seeking a firmer touch from him. Soon my bra straps were pushed from my shoulders, both breasts covered in the remnants of his kisses.

When he finally cupped me through my yoga pants, his fingers gripping me and feeling the wetness that I knew had soaked through, I bucked up into his hand. It wasn't going to be long before he got me to completely unravel. He shushed me, though I wasn't sure why, then kissed me softly. Was I speaking in tongues? I guess it was possible.

"Relax. I'll get you there. Promise."

"I can't wait, O. Please."

He ignored my plea and began kissing my neck again. The hand between my legs moved up as I groaned in protest, which was quickly replaced with a moan of approval as his hand slipped into my pants and under my panties. Slowly his fingers roamed over my already parted lips. He teased me as he touched me everywhere but my clit.

I cried out in ecstasy as a finger slipped inside me and circled me. "Oh God, O. I don't think I can take it."

Against my lips he told me, "You can. Relax, Des. Let me take care of you. There's no rush."

Take care of me. I liked the sound of that. A lot. His lips pulled a nipple to his mouth as his other hand began fucking me. My hips sought to greet every thrust of his hand and then his thumb began to tease my clit. I tried moving to a seated position, but could barely manage it. His arm circled my back, pulling me into his broad chest. My hands gripped the cushion on the couch as his other hand brought me closer to the edge. My back stiffened and I knew it was coming. Blurry vision took over for a split second before.

"O, kiss me."

"I want to watch you. I'll kiss you after."

I couldn't hold myself up any longer and sprawled back across his lap, my breasts thrust in the air. "Now...I'm...O!" The hand at my back pulled gently on my hair causing my back to arch more.

I could feel his breath on my face as he urged me on. Whispering, his sexy baritone filled my ears as he said the sexiest and most ridiculous thing to me. "Show me your O face, Des."

My eyes locked with his as I rode out the sensations, my moans turned into a silent cry from lips that were now swollen from his kisses. Everything from my toes up to the hair on my head was tingling. My nipples ached, they were so hard. The pulsing slowed and he resumed kissing my breasts as my body trembled at his touch. Just when I was about to chastise him for not kissing me, his lips met mine. The kiss was passion filled, a spark renewed inside me as I held his face close to mine.

"That was the sexiest thing I've ever seen."

I felt the blush spread across my cheeks as I shook my head at him. "I find that doubtful."

"Don't. It was. You were totally lost in my touch. I can't wait to do it to you again." I realized his fingers still occupied my pussy as he gently moved them. Without consent, my hips rose up and he smiled at me. "I think you like that idea."

It took all my strength, but I managed to sit up and then straddled his lap. "I do, but what about you?" I settled myself against the bulge in his jeans and kissed his lips as his hands ran up and down my back. "I want to see *your* O face!"

Lowering my hand, I cupped his erection and just as quickly he pulled my hand away. "What about me? I'm fine." My eyes popped open in confusion as I searched his hazel globes. "This was about you. Besides, call me old fashioned. I don't want to move too fast, Des."

Sitting back, I was mildly annoyed. "You just finger-fucked me on my couch. We surpassed fast about thirty minutes ago."

Smiling devishly—I wasn't sure if I wanted to kiss him or hit him— he remained calm and softly said, "I enjoyed every second of it, more than you know. But, I'm not going any further with you tonight. Not until you agree to one thing." My brows furrowed as I wondered what he was getting at. "You're not too old for me and I want to take you on a date."

Crossing my arms I clarified things for him. "That's *two* things, not one. I'll agree to the date, but being too old for you will have to wait."

He pursed his lips as his eyes moved to my mouth. "Fine. I accept. For now."

Unaware of what he was doing until it was too late, I squealed in fear—more for him, not me. "O, put me down. Your leg!"

He was now standing as I clung to his body. "My leg is fine. You're not *that* heavy." He started laughing as he walked toward my bedroom. "You need to sleep and so do I." He set me on my bed and started to leave the room.

"You're not staying?"

"I'm not going anywhere but to the couch." I started to object when he just shook his head and closed the door behind him. "Patience grasshopper."

"YOU'RE INFURIATING." I bellowed from my spot on the bed.

"JUST THE WAY YOU LIKE IT."

Groaning, I threw a pillow at the door and heaved myself back on the bed. A smile immediately spread across my face. I was in deep fucking shit with this one.

~ DESIREE ~

~ CHAPTER 5 ~

The next morning I woke to breakfast being made. He was in the kitchen cooking in nothing but his jeans and a wife-beater tank top. I couldn't keep my eyes off his arms as the muscles moved and flexed while he flipped pancakes. When I finally managed to pull my eyes from his body, I found his eyes on my face. I'd been caught red handed checking him out.

Winking, "Morning. Sleep good?"

Had I ever. Probably the best night's sleep I'd had in ages. "I did. You?"

"Your couch is comfy. If it wasn't I would've joined you." His attention went back to the stove and I sat down at the breakfast bar and imagined him joining me in bed. The clank of a plate startled me and brought me back to the present. "Eat up!"

When I was done eating, he leaned over and kissed me. It was an amazing kiss. Slow, sensual, and full of tongue. He tasted like syrup and I continued to lick at his lips looking for more of the sweetness. His hands moved to cup my face as he pulled his lips from mine. I was hot and bothered and would willingly let him spread me across the counter if he tried.

He left shortly after talking about clients he had at the gym. Turns out he was working as a personal trainer at one of the few gyms some of his brothers owned. That helped explain his amazing arms. He kissed me on the cheek and said he'd be in touch.

Almost a week passed. It took all my will power not to text him first. Especially since my dreams had been filled with him. It was ridiculous how consumed with him my thoughts had been. Then thinking about that made me paranoid and convinced me that he didn't feel the same way. I mean, who does what he did to me on the couch and then doesn't take what's his? Then that kiss after breakfast had me whirling, too. I'd offered myself to him like a sacrificial lamb and he'd turned me down without a second thought. Spouting some bullshit about being old fashioned and wanting to take it slow.

This was the problem with younger men. They were either consumed with putting notches in their belts or didn't have a fucking clue what they wanted. Gah! One minute I was thinking about the things I wanted to do to him and the next I was convincing myself I didn't want anything to do with him.

I nearly jumped out of my skin when my cell phone began buzzing. It was O. To answer or not to answer. On the fourth ring I caved and frantically slid the green button across the phone, hoping I wasn't too late.

Deep breath, "Hello?"

"Hey, Des. It's me."

"Hi. Who's me?"

"O." I remained silent. "Odysseus. Odysseus Kerrigan."

With a questioning tone, I repeated his name. "Odysseus, Odysseus?"

"Dammit, Des. Stop fucking with me."

I couldn't contain my laughter. "Admit it. I had you going for a second."

"Nope."

"You lie!" I heard him chuckle and waited to see what he'd say next.

"So, about that date."

"Hmm."

"Well?"

"Odysseus Kerrigan, for someone so old fashioned you sure aren't familiar with how to ask a girl out on a proper date."

I heard him take a deep breath. "Dammit." Now I felt bad. "Des, I'm sorry. Would you do me the honor to join me for dinner Friday night?"

"I'm sorry. I was just giving you a hard time. I'd love to join you for dinner."

"You're infuriating."

"That's what you like about me!"

"Yes, yes it is. Can I pick you up at six?"

"I have to work late Friday. Make it seven and I'll make sure I'm ready."

"Deal. I'll pick you up at your place at seven." He paused and then confessed, "I've missed you and I'm looking forward to seeing you again."

With a smile across my face and inside my heart, I reciprocated his sentiment. "Me too. See you Friday, O."

I disconnected the call and ran to my closet. It was already Wednesday and I needed to figure out what to wear. It dawned on me that this would be my first real date in almost two years. My routine of sleeping with men, not dating them, had become a normal I was happy to leave behind.

Friday was another normal day, but as the end of the work day approached, time seemed to move at a snail's pace. When I got home, I threw the mail on the table by the door, dropping my purse and keys, before heading further inside. I was so excited for my date with O that the feeling that something was off didn't even register with me until it was too late.

"Hey there, Buttercup." My heart stopped and my skin crawled. How had he gotten inside? Immediately all the things O had warned me about rang in my ears. Security system, cameras, deadbolts. "You're looking good. In a hurry to go somewhere?"

What did I say? I didn't want to endanger O, but I was scared for my own safety, too. Maybe Saul would leave if I told him I was expecting someone. Who was I kidding? I knew better than that.

"Nope, just relieved to be home so I can start the weekend."

Glancing around my bedroom, nothing seemed out of place. My gun was in the closet and I didn't think there was any way to get to it without him stopping me. Looking to the clock I had an hour before O was supposed to pick me up. An hour too long.

He stood up and took a few steps toward me as I backed away. "Wh, what are you doing here, Saul? You know you're not supposed to be here."

Smirking he replied, "It's been too long since I've tasted my Buttercup." My stomach convulsed in revulsion.

I tried another tactic, sympathy, when his fingers slithered down my cheek. Leaning in to his touch, I lied, "I don't want you to get in trouble. You know how that detective is."

"Missed me have you? Kiss me, Buttercup." His eyes narrowed in on mine as I forced myself to make eye contact with him. Lifeless brown eyes sneered back at me and I couldn't begin to fathom the crazy that laid behind them. I kissed his cheek and he sniggered, "You can do better than that."

My eyes were downcast, trying to take in his appearance when his fingers roughly gripped my chin, pulling my face up to his. "Please, Saul." I was desperate and grasping at straws. "It's that time of the month. I don't feel well."

"You forget that Aunt Flo never bothered me. That was you." Remembering that I had once been intimate with this demented man willingly, had my stomach revolting. Of course I didn't really know who I was dealing with then. I did now. "Get undressed." It wasn't a request.

It wouldn't be the first time he'd forced himself on me. There was no point in fighting, he'd just make it worse. Then I felt the vibration of my phone, alerting me of a text message. Saul didn't seem to hear it or he didn't care. It was probably O letting me know he was on his way. O. I was betraying him by *not* trying to resist Saul. I had to fight, but I couldn't let O come here. There was no telling what Saul's reaction would be.

Turning toward the closet where I knew my gun was, I asked Saul what he wanted. "Satin or lace?" His fingers came down on my wrist and yanked me back toward him. "I have new negligees. Don't you want to see them?"

"I told you to undress. Lingerie can wait till next time."

I was on the bed naked as Saul inspected my body. The room was freezing even with the heat blasting through the vents. There was a knock on my apartment door and Saul drew back, turning his head he glared at me. "Just ignore it, Saul."

"Who is it?"

If he knew it was a man I was interested in, things would just get worse. "A friend, a patient. He's having a hard time since returning home. I'm just trying to help him." Another knock came.

Leaning in closer, his sour breath filled my nostrils, "Get rid of him."

"I, can I have a robe or something? Please, Saul. You don't want him to see me naked do you?"

He yanked the robe down off my door and threw it at me. "Hurry up." I slid the robe around my body as he warned me, "Don't try anything, Desiree. Be a good girl." I just nodded before leaving the room.

The walk from my bedroom to the front door was one of the longest of my life. I wanted so badly to sprint to the door, to safety, to O. But was I willing to risk O's safety? He was bigger than Saul, he could take him, but Saul had my gun. He'd pulled it out of the back of his pants and waved it at me after I'd sat down on the bed. I couldn't risk O's life. Now, what to tell him to get rid of him. The tears were already threatening, my throat ached with unshed tears, and my body trembled.

Opening the door a crack, I peered out at him. He was holding a bouquet of flowers in various shades of white and pink. They were beautiful.

"You're not ready. I know I'm early. Sorry." He went to take a step toward me and I cowered back. His brows narrowed as he apologized again. "Sorry. I shouldn't have assumed you got my text. It was rude of me..."

"O, please. I can't go out with you tonight." My chest constricted as I said it, but it had to be done.

"I, uh, I don't understand." His eyes ran the length of my body and then he asked, "Are you not feeling well? Can I get you anything?"

"Jesus! Stop being so nice and dense." He flinched at my words and the tone I used. I had to hurt him. It was the only way. "I'm fine, just a little preoccupied." I fingered the sash of my satin robe as I shrugged my shoulders. "He showed up last night and we..."

He looked crushed and then I saw the anger as he spit out, "He who? What the hell is going on, Des?"

"An old flame, no one we've talked about," that was mostly true. I hadn't discussed Saul with him. "He was here when I got home from work last night, and, well, I didn't go in to work." The knife was already in, time to turn it, "We've been in bed all day."

O took a step back, running his fingers through his tousled hair. He stood there a second, not making eye contact. I caught the slight shake of his head as he took another step back, the flowers now hanging at his side. He started to speak and then shut his mouth before turning away and walking toward the elevator.

"I'm sorry. I didn't mean to hurt you." I meant those words. If only he knew what was really happening.

His free hand just flew up in the air, waving me off as he shouted, "Have a nice life, Des."

I couldn't bear to watch him get in the elevator and closed the door. Finally someone had sparked a hope inside me, a spark of happily ever after, of finding love after thirty. That spark was O. Now it was gone, he was gone. The tears were pouring down my face and I didn't realize it until their saltiness wetted my lips. I was about to reopen the door and run for my life when Saul appeared in front of me. The scream I started to let out was muted the minute his fist met my face.

~ DESIREE ~

~ CHAPTER 6 ~

I still don't talk about what happened over the next thirty six hours. It'd happened before and we all had our ways of coping. This time, I didn't call the cops. They couldn't protect me—hadn't protected me—and I wasn't ready to let them prove that again. Saul let me live which only meant one thing; he'd be back and I'd be ready. The only problem was I never knew if it'd be a day, a week, a month, or a year.

I took the next week off work, siting a family emergency, but knowing it was because even the best makeup couldn't hide all the bruises. By Tuesday I'd already signed back up for kickboxing, had cameras installed, and changed the locks. Tomorrow I would get back to the range and possibly invest in a new pistol. Of course a shotgun sounded good too. Surely that would blow a hole in him big enough to kill him.

Wednesday evening I was soaking in the tub, my new shotgun only an arm's length away, when someone began pounding on my front door. I flew out of the tub, water splashing everywhere. I ran through to my bedroom and made sure the door was locked. Yes, I'd had a deadbolt put on my bedroom door as well.

"Des! I know you're in there. Your car's in the lot. Please open up. I need to talk to you."

It was O. My body immediately ached for him. He'd tried calling earlier in the day, but sent no text. I couldn't see him. If I saw him there was a good chance I'd never let him out of my sight again. He was a good man; that much I knew, even if I'd only spent a handful of occasions with him. And I wanted him, I couldn't deny it

"I'll kick down the door, Des. You have ten seconds!" He couldn't be serious. What had him so suspicious? Then I heard him start to count down. "Ten! Nine! Eight!"

He wasn't going to kick down my door...was he? Surely the neighbors would call the cops. Shit, not a single person had called over the weekend and there were a few times I was certain someone would with the fight I was putting up with Saul.

BAM! "Three!"

"Fuck." I unbolted my bedroom door after putting on my robe, leaving the shotgun on the bed, and rushed to the front door. I began opening the front door just as he bellowed 'ONE'.

"Have you lost your mind, O?"

He just stared at me, his lips parted as he panted, and his eyes scrunched together as he looked over my face. My face. Shit. I lowered it, my hand at my brow. I wasn't even sure if he saw the bruises.

"Des, what's going on? I called work on Monday and you weren't there. Called again yesterday. Same thing. Today I stopped in. The girls confirmed that you *were* at work on Friday, but you had an emergency to tend to this week. Why did you lie to me?"

I was at a loss for words. I wanted to throw myself in his arms, but I had to get him to leave. I couldn't involve him. Trying to close the door, he immediately stuck his foot in the jamb, stopping me. My eyes darted to his face and that's when I knew he saw the bruises. His face paled and then he shoved past me and into my apartment.

"Where is he?" He disappeared into my bedroom and emerged with the shotgun. Holding it up with one hand, he pointed at it with the other as he asked, "What the fuck, Des?" I shut the front door, locking it before leaning against it. My legs quickly gave way as I curled into myself on the floor. He was at my side immediately. His voice was soft and full of concern, "I'll fucking kill him."

"Not if I do first."

He scooped me up and set me down in his lap on the couch. "Des, we need to call the police." My head on his shoulder, I just shook my head in refusal. "What do you mean 'No'? They need to know what happened." He took a deep breath. "Jesus. What happened?"

"I can't, O. I can't let it happen again and I can't tell you. I'll kill myself before he hurts me again."

The tears rolled down my cheeks as I felt his fingers under my chin. He traced the bruises gently and apologized over and over again. "This is my fault. He was here on Friday wasn't he? Why didn't you say something? I would've protected you."

Sobbing and with big breaths I cried out, "I couldn't risk you getting hurt. I still can't." I tried climbing off his lap as I continued babbling, "You should leave. I have to keep you safe."

Pulling me back to his lap he announced, "That's *my* job." He grew quiet as I burrowed into the safety and warmth of his body. "I'm so sorry, Des. I knew something was off, but, I...Fuck! I'm an idiot."

A long time passed, I may have even fallen asleep on him. It was easy to do considering the lack of sleep I'd gotten over the past five days. His hands were wearing a path over my back as I risked looking to his face. We didn't speak, almost as if no words needed to be said. He stroked my face and kissed my forehead before resting his own against it. I needed to hold him closer, believe he was real, and so I wrapped my arms around his neck and clung to him with all I had.

Softly in my ear I heard his tender words, "I can't believe I almost lost you. I can't get you out of my head, Des. Believe me, I tried." His hands were running through my hair and then cupping my neck, pressing me closer. "I shouldn't be talking like this. It's the last thing you need."

"It's everything I need. I need you, O and it scares me to death. I've never needed anyone."

Pulling back he cupped my face between his hands, "I need you, too. I know it's too soon, but fuck it. I'm falling for you, Des."

My voice shook as I admitted to him, "I'm falling too, O."

I knew he wanted to kiss me and I wanted to kiss him, but he was hesitant and I understood why. Pulling him closer, I took the lead and placed my lips against his. It was a soft, tender, and sweet kiss with very little tongue. Removing my lips from his, I hugged him tightly again.

"Des, have you seen a doctor? You could have serious injuries."

"No, but I'm ok."

"Des! I, shit, I don't, did he? I mean, you should probably get tested."

"I have an appointment tomorrow."

"Can I please convince you to talk to the cops? I'll come with you. They need to know. This fucker needs to be locked up. And, you're not staying here." He set me down next to him like I was a small child and stood up. Walking to the front door, he opened it and peered into the hallway. "I see you got cameras. Were they here Friday?"

"No. I just had them installed."

He exhaled sharply. "New locks." He walked back to my bedroom. "Shit, you put a lock here, too? Guess that makes sense. Yup, let's go. Pack your things."

"O, I'm not leaving."

"The fuck you aren't. There's no way in hell I'm letting you stay here. Alone or with a platoon of soldiers. Not. Happening." He sat back down next to me. "He's proven you're not safe here. I can't let you sit here like bait. Please, Des. See reason."

I knew he was right. "I don't have anywhere to go."

Tilting his head, he half smiled at me. "Um, hello? You can stay with me."

"I don't know. I, I thought you wanted to take things slow?" He just looked at me. "I promised myself I wouldn't live with a man ever again unless we were married." He was still smirking and I felt embarrassed. "I know it's silly. It's just..."

"You've been burned one too many times?"

"Yes. I can call my cousin. I'm sure she'll let me crash on her couch."

"Nope. Not happening. I have two bedrooms if that'll make you more comfortable."

I didn't want a separate bedroom from him, but having my own meant we weren't living together, not like that. "Umm, I guess that could work."

~ DESIREE ~

~ CHAPTER 7 ~

I agreed to go to the police station the next day as long as O went with me, knowing what they'd ask me to do and knowing it'd be pointless. I needed his support and he gave it tenfold. We packed my bags and drove to his apartment, leaving my car behind for now. He showed me around his place. It was similar in size to mine, but not as updated, though he had two bedrooms.

That first night as he moved some things out of his bedroom, I pleaded with him, "O, this isn't necessary. I can take the other room."

"Yes it is. We're taking this slow. You need time."

I walked over to him and wrapped my arms around his waist. "Thank you. For everything."

"You don't need to thank me. I'd give you the world if I could."

"I'm beginning to believe that."

He kissed the top of my head before pulling back. "You should get some sleep."

I just nodded and watched him walk out of the bedroom. I could hear him shuffling around in the room next door and wondered what he was doing. Not wanting to pry, I just closed the door and sat down on his bed. Pulling a pillow to my chest, I inhaled his scent and rolled to my side.

When I woke, the overhead light had been turned off, but a nightlight shone in the corner, and a blanket covered me. I got undressed and searched my bag for something to wear when I spotted a clothes hamper. The clothes were probably dirty and I didn't care. Digging through, I quickly found a t-shirt and when I held it to my nose, I knew it would be perfect. Slipping it over my naked torso, it hung just below my panties. I crawled under the covers and laid there for what seemed like hours.

Sighing, I grabbed my phone off the night stand and scrolled through my playlist. I settled on Lana Del Ray's *Young And* Beautiful and replayed it over and over. The song easing some worries and making others worse. Would he still love me when I was pushing fifty and him barely forty? I was being absurd. Eventually sleep found me, Lana still singing me to sleep.

The next morning I woke to a scuffle happening at the foot of my bed.

"Jesus! Get off of me, O. What the fuck?"

I was sitting up, clutching the blankets under my chin as I saw a bare chested O reach his arm out to someone. Another tanned and muscled arm grabbed his and soon two totally different, yet equally gorgeous men stood in front of me.

The stranger looked to me and smiled. "Sorry. I didn't realize my brother had company. He's not one to entertain the ladies as of late." His eyes roamed my body, like he could see what was under the covers. "Seems to me that's changed and I can see why." O grabbed him by the back of the shoulders and pushed him from the room as his brother laughed.

"Shut up, Will." The door closed and I exhaled, finally able to breathe again. The door cracked open again and O smiled at me. "Sorry. I kind of have an open door policy with my brothers. That'll change today."

"It's ok. Just frightened me." I looked to the clock. "Wow. It's late.

"I'm going to make some breakfast. Any requests?"

"Coffee?"

"I hooked up your Keurig. It's waiting for you." It was the one small appliance I insisted on bringing. Never left home without it. He winked at me and then nodded toward the bathroom. "It's small, but there's towels in there. We should head out soon."

"Ok." I smiled and he shut the door. Climbing out of bed, I walked into the bathroom. He was right. It was small, but it would work just fine.

When I got out of the shower, my phone blaring music in the small bathroom, I'll admit I did some snooping. I don't know what I was looking for, but all I found was what anyone would expect to find. Razors, shaving cream, toothpaste, deodorant, and other things a man would have. No condoms. I shrugged it off. He probably kept them elsewhere. He was right anyway. I wasn't quite ready for that no matter how my body reacted to his. Thank God my mind was great at compartmentalizing.

Pulling the towel from my head, my hair cascaded down my back in tangled waves. I hung the discarded towel on the back of the door and walked back into the bedroom. *Replay* by Zendaya started playing and I couldn't help but move to the beat. Pulling the other towel from my body, I lifted my legs one at a time to the side of the bed and dried them off. My arms were next as my hips swayed back and forth. When I turned around my eyes landed on him.

Jumping back I gasped, "Shit!" Clutching the towel to my chest, I tried covering up.

His eyes traveled up my body and locked on my eyes. "Music's a little loud, don't you think?" Then he smirked.

Shaking my head, "Nope. I like it loud." I wrapped the towel around me and his eyes didn't drift from mine once. He took a step toward me as I swallowed hard. "Did you need something?"

Leaning around me, my heart pounding in response to him being so near, he opened the chest of drawers behind me. "Clothes." He waved some fabric in front of me that I didn't quite make out before turning toward the door.

Then it dawned on me that he took clothes out the night before. "What happened to the clothes you took out of here last night?" Turning to look at me, his eyes full of mischief, he just smiled and shrugged his shoulders. "Do I need to worry that you're a voyeur, O?"

He chuckled and responded, "With you?" His eyes moved over my body and then back to my eyes. "Most definitely." My knees grew weak and it took all I had not to collapse on the bed or throw myself at him. "Breakfast's ready. I'm going to shower." The door closed and I dropped to the bed.

After dressing I made my way to the kitchen and stopped dead in my tracks. His brother, I think he said his name was Will, was sitting at the small kitchen table. O could've warned me. I took a deep breath and walked past him, straight for the Keurig. I popped a kcup in and waited.

"So, Des is it?" I turned to look at him, smiling softly. He wore glasses, had a light stubble, his hair was styled perfectly, unlike O's unkempt hair, and he was just as hot. Muscles pulled at the fabric of his too tight shirt.

"Yes. Will?" He stood and shook my hand, nodding.

"Aren't you a little old for my brother?" *What the fuck?* I'm certain my eyes nearly popped from my head at the question. My mouth burst open for a response and closed again.

Finally, I said, "Age is just a number."

He studied me and had the nerve to tell me he didn't care. "I don't care. O already told me. I just want him to be happy. He hasn't stopped talking about you the past couple weeks, maybe longer."

Will didn't say anything more. Was he warning me? I wasn't quite sure and before I had a chance to ask, O reappeared. He looked to me and back to Will and it was like he knew what had transpired.

"Lay off, Will." Will lifted his hands in surrender and took a drink of his coffee. O walked over to me and kissed the top of my head. "Did you sleep ok?" I nodded and turned back to my coffee which was now done.

Will left a few minutes later, confirming he was going to take care of O's clients for the next few days. When I got in O's truck I started to grow nauseous knowing where we were headed. He got behind the wheel and took my hand in his. He didn't need to say anything, just having him there was enough. We headed toward the police station.

A rape kit was taken at my doctor's office, though we all knew it wouldn't show what we needed it to. They also did a urine pregnancy test, which was negative, and an STD test. She drew blood to send in for an HIV test as well as to check for pregnancy. I knew the blood test could catch it sooner than a pee stick would. The detective put an APB out for

Saul and got all of O's information so he'd know where I was. He chastised me for waiting so long, but said he understood. Promising that they'd find Saul, O and I left.

"You hungry?"

"Yeah, but can we make something or just pick something up?"

"Of course."

We were having dinner later that weekend with Stacey. I wanted her to meet O and I needed to update her. She didn't even know the name of the man I now had in my life. We were sitting at a booth in O'Grady's when I saw her walk in. When she spotted us, she stopped short and stared at O. Oh God, they knew each other? It was written all over both their faces.

"O? Des? I, what's going on?" She sat down across from us and looked straight at us.

"You two know each other?" I looked to O, who seemed uncomfortable and then to Stacey. "Someone better tell me what the hell is going on right now."

"Calm down, Des. It's not what you think." He tried to pull me closer as I turned to face him in the booth.

"Not what I think? Because I think you and my cousin know each other in an intimate way." My envy was sprouting up like a nasty little weed. "If you and she have a history, I don't think I can do this."

Stacey started cracking up as I glowered at her. She was shaking her head as she testified, "Des, I know O, but not like you think. Calm down. My best friend Lucy is married to his brother Heath."

She was covering. I looked at O. There was more, but he wasn't saying anything. Glaring at Stacey I leaned in toward her and spit out, "There's more. What is it?"

"Shit." That came from O. "Listen, Des," I wasn't going to like the sound of this, "Stacey and I went on a few dates, nothing more."

"When?"

"That's not important."

"The fuck! Yes it is."

"Jesus, Des. Can we talk about this later?"

I wasn't sure the extent of their relationship, if you could call it that, but I was heartbroken. Every crazy scenario running through my mind. I knew I needed to calm down, but I also needed to know what I was dealing with.

I took a deep breath, "I need to know. One of you better spill it."

Stacey started talking. "We met up a little over a month ago. Just dinner and drinks. Nothing happened."

I believed her, but he'd said a few dates. "You said a few. When was number two?"

"Last weekend." My eyes burned into the side of his face and when he finally made eye contact with me, a single tear fell from his eye. "Des..."

"Did you fuck her?"

"He tried." My head jerked toward Stacey. What did she mean 'he tried'?

"Jesus, Stacey. I was drunk."

"You weren't that drunk."

I started pushing O out of the booth and he wouldn't budge. I looked at him and growled out, "If you don't let me out of this booth, I'll climb over it."

"You can't leave, Des."

"I'd leave if I was her, too."

"Stacey! You're not helping." I turned back to O, "Please, I'll be back. I just need to go to the bathroom." He studied my eyes and then got out of the booth. As I walked past him, his fingers brushed mine.

I was leaning over the sink in the bathroom taking deep breaths. Stacey and I weren't as close as we'd once been and it wasn't the first time we'd had disagreements over a man. I was replaying everything over in my head. 'He tried' to sleep with her. What the hell did that mean? And on Friday, after I'd dismissed him. A sob broke from my chest. If I'd told him I was in danger, or done something, he wouldn't have ended up with Stacey last Friday night. He was supposed to be with me.

"Des, I'm sorry." I wiped at my face and stared at Stacey. "It shocked the shit out of me to see you two sitting there all chummy. Shit, I don't know what to say. I've been crushing on him for a long time. To see him with you just hit a nerve."

I shook my head, "I didn't know. It's been so long since we've really talked." I didn't know what to do. "Saul came back."

"What?"

"Friday night I was supposed to go out with O. When he showed up, I hurt him to get rid of him because Saul was there."

"He's a sick fuck. Are you ok?"

"I can't. It was bad. O, Stacey, O and I..."

She nodded and smiled. "I get it. It's ok. Why didn't you tell him about Saul? I mean, I know *why* you didn't but..."

I spewed the words before I even knew what I was saying. "I'm falling in love with him, Stacey. I don't think I can stop it. There's something so powerful between us, like nothing I've ever felt."

"He's a good guy. I'm a little jealous. But nothing happened between us, not really. Just don't tell me how amazing he is in bed. I may jump off a cliff. Lord knows he's hung."

I just smiled as I wiped at my drying tears. She didn't need to know that we hadn't had sex, yet. It was no one's business but ours.

~ DESIREE ~

~ CHAPTER 8 ~

We finished dinner with Stacey, but she didn't hang out long. Driving back to O's place was slightly uncomfortable and I couldn't take the silence any longer. After Stacey and I had talked in the bathroom, O and I didn't have a chance to talk so the news of him and Stacey still hung heavy in the air between us.

"O, we should talk."

"Des, I'm so sorry. I was so upset that night. I ran into Stacey and..."

I squeezed his thigh and reassured him, "O, its ok. We're good. Stacey told me. I don't blame you." He covered my hand with his own. "You had every right to be furious with me that night. You know, I found the flowers in the hallway. No one had bothered to clean them up. You gave them quite the beating. You'll never know how much I regret what I did."

"*You* didn't do anything."

I leaned in and kissed him. Before it became too heated, I asked him, "Do you dance?"

"I've been known to, but that was before. I think I'm limited to slow dancing now."

"I'd love to slow dance with you."

"Up with you then." He walked to the sound bar by his TV and motioned for my phone. "Pick a song or five."

I pulled up some songs and handed him the phone. Plugging it in, he walked to the center of the room and held out his hand. I took it and let him pull me close. *Broken Ones* by Jacquie Lee played. We were both definitely broken, but I was pretty confident that he'd take my broken pieces and make them whole again. I just prayed I could do the same for him, though he seemed much more put together than I was.

"Fuck, this song is depressing."

I squeezed my arm around his waist tighter, "Not really. We're all broken in some fashion."

He pushed me back to look at me, "Des, you're not broken."

"With you I don't feel broken. I feel like I finally have a chance to be whole again."

He placed his forehead on mine, "Me too."

"O, please kiss..."

I didn't get a chance to finish my request before his lips seized mine. His hands were in my hair as he held my head in place. Slowly, his tongue slid across my lips, causing a tremor to pass through me. Thank the heavens I could still feel that. My hands moved under his shirt, desperate after all this time to feel his warm skin. My fingers moved over the muscles of his back and I gently dug my nails into his broad shoulders.

"Des, we should stop this."

"Please, O. All I want is to feel you, nothing else." I took his hand and led him to the bedroom. Kicking my shoes off, I stripped my jeans down my legs as he stared at me.

"Des?" He was being cautious and I understood. I could see the bulge pushing against his jeans and watched as he adjusted himself. "You're not making this easy."

Beaming, I pulled him closer. I sat down on the bed and moved up, lying in the middle of it. Pulling his shirt off, he dropped it to the floor and crawled next to me. We kissed for a long time, his hands only roaming my face, arms, belly, and legs.

Without warning or permission, Saul invaded my thoughts. I tried shaking it off. O's hand finally lingered near my panties and a shiver swept over me and not the good kind. My whole body tensed and I felt him remove his hand from me.

"Des. Talk to me."

My hands immediately covered my face as I tried to hide the tears. He was right, I wasn't ready. Between broken breaths, I apologized, "I'm sorry. I'm not ready. I thought I was."

"Shhh. It's ok. We've both been through our share of trauma. Give it some time. I'm not going anywhere." I felt him get off the bed and cover me with the blankets. He sat down next to me and pulled my hands from my face. "Look at me." I did, barely. "You need some rest. I'll be right next door if you need me." I nodded and he kissed my forehead.

I was so embarrassed. He left the room and once the door closed, I curled into the fetal position. I woke a few hours later, shivering. I couldn't get warm and though I knew I wasn't ready to sleep with him, I needed him close.

Climbing out of bed I made my way to the guest room. The door was open and as my eyes adjusted, I saw his large figure sprawled out in the bed, making it look tiny. As I moved toward the bed, I had second thoughts. Waking a soldier with his history probably wasn't a good idea. I turned to leave when his voice caught me off guard.

"You need something?"

Turning back toward the bed, I stuttered, "I, just, sorry. I didn't mean to wake you."

"I wasn't asleep. I woke the minute you climbed out of bed."

Scoffing, "You did not hear me get up."

"Yes I did. It's what I'm trained for."

"Sorry." This was a mistake.

"What is it, Des?"

Spit it out! "I was cold, but I can go, do you have more blankets? I'll let you sleep." I stood there, waiting for the rejection I was sure would come, though not sure why I thought he'd reject me.

"Get your ass over here." He threw back the covers and I gingerly climbed in next to him. I lay down as close to him as I could, my body half hanging off the edge of the bed. "I thought you wanted me to hold you?"

"Well, you're not giving me much room."

"You're right, I'm not. You want to be closer to me, you're going to have to make that move. I'm comfortable and not budging."

Sighing, "You're infuriating."

"You like it that way."

I rolled to my side and put my head on his shoulder. His warmth immediately surrounded me. "Oh, God. You're like a furnace." I moved in closer, draping my free arm over his torso.

"You're like an icebox. Christ!"

"Wait till you feel these." I slid a foot up his leg and when the coldness reached his thigh, he jumped.

"You're not human. No one's feet are that cold." Laughing, I pulled them away as his arm came around my back. "Go to sleep, Des."

"Good night, O."

"Night."

The whole next week he either drove me to work or followed me and he was there waiting when I got out. His place was actually a shorter drive to work for me which was nice. I hadn't felt safer or more loved in my life.

Every night we'd go to our separate rooms just for me to crawl into bed with him a few hours later. I'd made some emergency appointments with my therapist and was feeling better. There was still no word on Saul. His apartment was empty and he'd stopped showing up to work. I tried not to think about it.

I climbed into bed feeling more content than I had in a long time. For the first time, O came to me that night, not the other way around. I jumped up at the sound of the door opening and just stared at him.

Fuck, he was sexy. His bare chest, ripped with muscles, and a smattering of hair. Sleep pants hung low on his hips and I was well aware of the wetness pooling in my panties. He climbed in next to me as I stared down at him.

"Can I help you?"

Smirking, he nonchalantly said, "Nope. Just missed my bed. And I feel like there should be no more separate rooms."

"You think so?" His eyes jerked toward mine as I laughed.

"Des?"

"Yes, O?"

"I don't want you to leave."

"I have to go home eventually. I can't stay here forever."

"Why not?"

My eyes drifted to his as I wondered what he was getting at. The truth was I didn't want to leave either, but I wasn't this girl was I? I didn't just move in with someone on a whim. "I told you, I don't want to live with someone until..."

"...Until you're married?" I just nodded in response. "You said it, not me."

What the hell was he talking about? He couldn't possibly mean what I thought he meant. "What?" I started laughing, "You want to get married? You don't even know me."

Sliding closer he started talking nonsense and I believed every word of it. "I know enough. Marry me, Des. I'll keep you safe. Nothing will ever happen to you again."

I was in shock and ecstatic. I was fucking crazy. "O, it's not funny. Be serious."

"I've never been more serious in my life. You make me feel things I never thought I'd feel again. I know it's the same for you, too. Deny it if you dare."

"I, fuck. Yes, I feel it too, but it's so soon. People will think we're insane."

"Fuck them. I am crazy. Crazy for you." He placed chaste kisses all over my face as I tried to talk myself out of saying yes. "I have something for you."

"You do?"

He sat up and turned on the lamp on the night stand. He opened his hand and lying in the palm of his hand was a diamond ring. "Desiree Greene, will you marry me?"

"O? It's for me?"

"Of course it is."

My tear filled eyes looked to his as I decided to follow my heart one more time. "Yes."

He beamed as he encouraged me, "Try it on." I held my finger out as he slid the cushion cut diamond onto my ring finger.

A tear fell down my cheek. "I love it." He laid us back down and pulled me to my spot on his chest and ran his hands up and down my back.

I hadn't met any of his family, except for Will, or any of his friends. And my parents, getting them here anytime soon would be unlikely given the distance. But, we were adults and I knew we didn't need their blessing to know how we felt.

~ DESIREE ~
~ CHAPTER 9 ~

"O, I know this will sound crazy, but I need to try again. I need to know I can let you...do things to me."

"Baby, there's no rush."

"I know, but...Please." I crawled on top of him and straddled his waist. Looking down on him, his hands resting on the pillow above his head, "Can we try again?"

His arms moved and stopped when he cupped my face. "I like you on top." He kissed me and whispered into my mouth, "You're in control. Use me, baby."

His words resonated with me. Maybe being on top and in charge was just what I needed. Removing his hands from my face, I pinned them above his head. Lowering my face, I kissed his chest and made my way up to his neck. We hadn't done this nearly enough. He could hardly contain himself as I sucked and nipped on his neck and ears. His hardness grew below me and I pressed into it, hitting just the right spot.

"Oh, God."

"Des, you're killing me."

My hand slid between our bodies as I shifted a little lower and finally held onto what I'd wanted to for so long. His length and girth were both impressive as I swirled his pre-cum around his tip. His hips bucked and he lifted himself to his elbows, watching me stroke him. I released him long enough to push his pants down his thighs and gripped him again.

He sat up and I avoided his kiss as I watched his face. His cock pulsed in my hands and I was enjoying this more than I thought I would. Burying his head in my neck, he began sucking. I moved closer to him at the same time he pulled me closer.

"Des, I want to touch you. Please tell me I can."

My clit throbbed in response to his words. "Yes. Just, oh, God."

"I'll go slowly."

His hand moved over my ass and squeezed, his fingers pushing under the lace fabric. I continued stroking him as his other hand moved under my shirt and found my breast. I cried out louder than I expected and had to assure him it was a good cry when he pulled back.

"Can I take it off?" He looked at the shirt of his that I'd been sleeping in every night and I nodded.

His fingers ran up my ribcage as I lifted my arms and pulled them out of the sleeves. Hazel-green eyes met mine as his hand ran over the top of my chest from shoulder to shoulder. I lowered my lips to his and found his cock once again. I moved my hips to press closer to him.

"Please, O. Touch me."

A grunt was his only response as he kissed my neck and I felt the palm of his hand cup me through my panties. I arched into his hand and he moved his fingers against me. Moving lower, the small scrap of fabric barely covered me and he easily pushed it aside. I was still stroking him. He was so close to my entrance, just a slight movement and we could be joined as one, but I didn't want to let go of him.

His fingers slid over my now exposed lips as he called my name, "Des." My eyes found his as he began working his fingers over my clit. "Just you and me, baby. I want to watch you come."

My eyes rolled back slightly and I smiled at him as he slid a finger inside. "I want to watch you come, too. Show me *your* O face."

We both laughed and resumed panting right after as we continued our joint assault on one another. Slowly, he slid a second finger inside me as I pulsed around him, knowing two fingers was nothing compared to what his cock would feel like. His fingers worked together and the thumb of his other hand found my clit. Leaning back, I held his cock, but it took all my will power to continue stroking him, lost in his touch.

"O, Odysseus. Please don't stop."

"Fuck, Des." He snarled out, "Look at me." I did. "Keep stroking me." I did. "Say it again."

"Odysseus." My thighs clenched and I knew I was close. "Please kiss me, Odysseus."

He sat back up but never missed a beat while finger-fucking me. "I can't say no when you say my name like that."

"Like what? Odysseus?" I knew what I was doing and so did he. "Right there."

I couldn't move my hand up and down his length anymore. My world imploded around his fingers and I couldn't breathe. When I thought I might pass out, he resuscitated me with his kiss as he fucked the hand I held him with. I took the kiss deeper and resumed stroking him, with more vigor than before, as he pulled every last tremor from my body.

"Des, I'm going to, oh shit."

"Come for me, Odysseus." I pulled his ear into my mouth and then bit his neck as he stiffened in my hand. His arms held me tight just before his orgasm conquered him. I slid my hand up and down, his seed covering every part of his cock and my hand. "You're going to kill me." His hand came down over mine, "You have to stop."

I just smiled and pecked his lips before giving him one more stroke. "I can't remember the last time I did that. Thank you."

"Thank *you*." He kissed me and then I climbed off his lap and headed to the bathroom to clean up. When I looked up into the bathroom mirror, he was towering behind me. Turning to face him he pulled me close. "You ok?"

"I'm perfect. Thank you."

I left the bathroom and crawled into bed. He sat down next to me and I recognized the sounds of him removing his prosthetic. When he lay down next to me, we curled into one another as had become our habit.

"Get some rest. We have a big day ahead of us tomorrow."

Yawning, "I'm already there."

A few days later, on St. Patrick's Day in the afternoon, we stood in front of a judge with a few dozen of our closest friends and family, mostly his, and said 'I do'.

We didn't know each other like we should, but we knew we were bonded in a way we couldn't explain. He got me, accepted me, loved me—though he hadn't said it yet—and I felt the same way. I'd never felt this way in my entire life about one single person.

We went to dinner that night with his family and our friends. His parents had made reservations at a local Irish Pub, and we had the back banquet room to ourselves. It was a gesture we weren't expecting, but were so thankful for.

His dad gave a toast and then thanked us for at least picking a great day to commit ourselves. "Love has its ups and downs. May the luck of the Irish always be on your side because Lord knows it's been on ours." O smiled at me and kissed me softly. We all raised our glasses in salute and then drank up.

I was chatting with Lucy, who I really liked, when his father interrupted us. I was looking forward to getting to know her and hoped to spend more time with her soon. Heath couldn't keep his hands off her. It was sweet.

"Now, my son has a song picked and would like to dance with is bride." My father-in-law walked over to us and kissed my cheek and then Lucy's. "Welcome to the family, Desiree. We're glad you're here." I looked over to where O had moved to stand, his mom and four brothers flanking him. His father followed the focus of my eyes and snickered, "They're a good bunch. We take care of our own."

Lucy agreed, "He's right. They're all amazing."

"I see that. I feel a little lost being an only child amongst all this rabble."

Lucy laughed and said, "You have NO idea!"

"Ha! Rabble it is." Music began to play as he said, "Your husband awaits my dear."

Nodding, I walked toward O. He wore slacks, a dress shirt and tie while I managed to find a dress. It was very simple, not the wedding dress I'd envisioned, but I loved it. My hair hung down my back in soft waves. He pulled me close, his fingers pulling gently on the ends of my hair.

"There's something you should know, Des."

"What's that?" I smiled up at him as I figured out the song that played, that he'd picked. *Look After You* by The Fray with its mellow piano and string melody serenaded us.

"I love you, Des. I don't expect you to say it back, but I had to tell you."

"I love you, too O."

We didn't stay too much longer. Eager to get home for many reasons. One being we both had to work the next day.

With our hearts on our sleeves and our guard down, we walked into the apartment that night not expecting to find what awaited us. The place had been tossed, or at least that was the impression that was meant to be left. O pulled out his cell and dialed 9-1-1. Opening the front closet, he pulled out the shotgun off the top shelf and loaded it. The sound it made had me cringing and I was oblivious to what he was saying into the phone.

The sound of glass breaking came from one of the bedrooms and he surged toward it after handing me the phone.

"O! Don't!" But he didn't listen.

The operator was talking to me, telling me that the cops were on their way. I was sobbing into the phone when I heard what sounded like a scuffle coming from the bedroom.

I heard the voice that filled my nightmares bellow out, "She's mine! I'll kill you both before I let you have her."

"She's MY wife, not yours."

Another crash filled my ears and I found myself cowering into the closet. I shut the door, slid to the floor and began rocking back and forth. Glass shattered and the sound of wood snapping filled my ears. The ruckus continued and like a coward I hid in the closet, paralyzed with fear.

Then my nightmare became worse. The sound of a gun going off rang through the air.

"No, no, no, no." I covered my mouth, trying to be silent as I heard Saul's voice again.

"Where you at, Buttercup?"

I decided then and there I would fight until he killed me. O would never let Saul get to me unless it was over his dead body. My heart shattered. Saul must've shot O, something I didn't anticipate.

The closet door swung open and I looked up to see Saul staring down at me. He reached for me with blood covered hands. Dragging me out by my hair, I clawed at his hands as he yanked me to my feet. When he had me nose to nose with him, I spit in his face. He sneered and licked the side of my cheek. With everything I had, I kicked him in the nuts. I turned back to the closet where I'd spotted crutches just before he'd pulled me out. At the same time, the sound of sirens filled the air. The cops were close.

"DES!" It was O.

Saul turned at the sound of O's voice and I took my aim. I bashed the end of the crutch against his face as hard as I could. He staggered back and I glanced O shuffling toward us. Blood dripped down the face of my groom and down his arm as he limped. He cocked the shotgun and aimed it at Saul, who was standing in front of me. I fell back down into the closet to take cover just as Saul pulled a gun from his own waistband.

"O! Look out!"

I was sobbing, my face buried in my hands. "Des, Des, its ok. I'm ok." I started lashing out at whoever it was that was trying to touch me. Hands gripped my shoulders and shook me, "DES!"

Looking up I didn't expect to see his hazel eyes staring back at me. "O?" I flung my arms around him and began sobbing.

"Shh. I got you."

"You're hurt. Where is he?"

"I'm ok. Just a scratch. I told you, I'd protect you with everything I had. I'll always look after you." He held me for several moments as I got my emotions and breathing back under control.

"Odysseus, Desiree, we have some questions for you."

I looked up into the eyes of the detective and knew this night wouldn't be over anytime soon. O squeezed my hand and helped me to my feet. "He needs to see a doctor. The questions can wait." O tried saying he was ok and I refused to hear it. "Now!"

"Des, I'm fine."

"So help me God, Odysseus. You've done your job, now let me do mine." He pursed his lips at me. "You protected me, now let me protect you. You need to see a doctor."

Another detective came walking up and announced, "Sir, he got away."

I felt O's entire body go stiff. "How the fuck did he get away? I shot him!"

"Son, we'll find him. If you shot him with that," he pointed at the shotgun on the floor, "he won't get far."

"No, no, no…"

O pulled me toward the kitchen and away from the detectives. "Des, look at me. He won't get to you."

"Don't you get it? He ALWAYS gets to me." He pulled me close as I choked out, "I'll never be safe. Not until he's dead, or I'm dead."

"If I have to kill him myself, I will. I promise you, he won't get to you again."

Sniffling, "You can try, but you can't promise. No one can."

"I'll protect you with my life. I'll never let anything happen to you again." He kissed me softly and pulled me close. "I'll give my body to protect yours."

I tried believing him, wanted to believe him. He was with me and together we'd get through this, but we had a long way to go. If I had to put a bullet in Saul myself I would. O was the only price I wasn't willing to pay. I knew O would do the same. His body, heart, and soul had become more precious to me than any other thing.

HEART

~ ODYSSEUS ~

~ CHAPTER 10 ~

I held her in my arms, staring at what was left of my apartment. The couch had been shredded, almost every dish was broken and lying on the kitchen floor, and there was blood smeared all over. Des hadn't even seen the bedroom yet, and I didn't want her to. The message scrawled on the bathroom mirror was enough to give *me* nightmares.

The EMS and Des both insisted that I go to the hospital to make sure it wasn't more than a mild concussion. I'd called Will and asked him to come to my apartment right away, that it was an emergency. He got there quicker than I thought he would, considering he originally thought I was joking.

Will walked in and looked to me and then Des, trying to take it all in. Her beautiful white dress had a few tears and streaks of red across it. She was curled into my side and still trembling, though I knew she'd deny it.

"Jesus. What the fuck? Are you ok?"

Des pleaded with Will immediately. "He's refusing to go to the hospital. Maybe you can convince him?" Des was over-reacting, but I loved her for it.

"I said I'd go. I just wanted to wait for Will. I'm not leaving you alone." Will understood. I'd filled him in on more of Des' past than I'm sure she would've liked, but it was for her protection.

"Do you want me to call Mom and Dad?"

"Not now. It can wait till morning. Can you drive us to the hospital?" Turning to Des, I whispered in her ear, "Baby, can you give me just a minute? I need to talk to Will."

Her fingers dug into my side as she tried to object, but she couldn't find the words.

"I'm not leaving Des, just going right over there." I pointed to the kitchen and she nodded. "You should let the EMS check you, just to make sure you're ok." She searched my eyes for a moment and then agreed.

Will and I took a few steps away as the EMS tech had Des sit in a chair in the living room. Will pulled my attention away, asking, "O, what happened?"

"We walked in and found the place this way. He was still here. I was an idiot. I heard glass shatter in the bedroom and found the window busted. It was a decoy and I fell for it."

"Dude, you're alive, she's alive. Sounds like you saved the day."

I ran my hands through my hair in frustration and then winced in pain, forgetting about the wound in my scalp. "Fuck! I fucking shot him and he got away."

"O, he could've killed you. You're lucky he didn't shoot you."

Snarling, I confessed, "He did." Will looked to me stunned as I clarified, "It's just a scratch. Listen, the bedroom is trashed. I don't want her going in there, not if I can avoid it. Can you try to find some clothes for her that haven't been trashed?" A sudden wave of dizziness took me over and Will braced me before I collapsed.

EMS and Des were at my side immediately. They decided to take me to the hospital immediately and Will swore he'd be right behind. I made it down the stairs with some assistance, my leg was killing me, and I was more worried about that than I was about my head. Though my worry for Des outweighed it all.

I watched her closely in the ambulance. The spark in her beautiful dark blue eyes wasn't there. There was a hardness to her, like a shadow had been cast upon her, something I'd only glimpsed once or twice when she tried shutting me out and it scared me. Not like I was scared of her, but scared of what that hardness would do to her. She was twirling her new ring and I reached for her hand.

She leaned in as close as she could as I promised her, "It's going to be ok."

She just smiled half-heartedly and then we pulled in to the hospital. They wheeled me back to the ER, Des right beside me. They ran a battery of tests and did a head CT after Des' persistence, worried I could have a brain bleed. Her med school training paying off. She was able to talk 'shop' with the docs and I was impressed.

Turned out there was no brain bleed, but I did have a pretty serious concussion. My leg was also X-rayed, but nothing was found. Just some bad bruising.

"We're going to let you go home, but you need to take it easy. No vigorous activity for at least five days."

"Doc, I'm a personal trainer."

"Not this week you aren't. That leg and your head need a break. Don't watch too much TV or do too much reading. Spend as much time as you can relaxing in bed." The doc glanced at Des and back to me. With a grin on his face, "I know you just got married, but you should abstain, too. Go see your doc if your symptoms don't ease up in the next couple days." DICK! He was getting pleasure from this. He signed a few papers and informed us, "You can get dressed. We'll get you out of here ASAP."

As the doc left, Will walked in with three coffees. He couldn't deal with sitting in the room and had probably been running laps around the hospital while I was having my tests run. It was nearly dawn and coffee was a blessing and a curse at this point. All I wanted to do was sleep and I'm sure Des felt the same way. Des had already changed her clothes, her ruined dress now wadded up in the duffle bag.

She helped me get out of my gown as Will sat in the chair, playing on his phone. Sitting on the edge of the bed, in nothing but my underwear, she helped me pull a shirt over my head. Her hands tenderly smoothed the shirt over my chest before she let out a small whimper.

"I almost lost you." She was sobbing in her hands as she choked out, "He shot you, because of me."

It turned out to be more than a scratch. The bullet from his gun had gone clean through my shoulder, a miracle in itself. "No, he shot me because he's crazy." I tried soothing her and it just seemed to bring more out of her. I looked to Will who just nodded and left the room giving us some privacy.

"How did he get away? I know I was there, but you shot him. He could be anywhere." She was nearly hysterical.

"Des, you need to calm down. The police will find him. He needs medical attention and he can't just get that anywhere."

She started shaking her head vigorously. "Yes, yes he can."

"What do you mean?" We hadn't discussed Saul in any great detail, but I had a feeling we were about to.

"He's a surgeon, a doctor. That's how we met. He was hurt in a car accident and I was his therapist."

With those simple words everything became so clear, like the fog had been lifted. Saul was the former patient and the reason why she had been reluctant to date me. It was probably more of a reason than her concern of being too old for me.

"Des, I had no idea."

I was trying to remain calm, her own nerves clearly shot. I didn't know what else to say. Her head was resting on my chest and as her breathing started to normalize the nurse came in with the discharge papers. The nurse didn't say anything, but Des heard the curtain open. Turning her back, she wiped at her face and then faced me again, faking a smile. She helped me with my pants and then put my shoes on. Will was waiting in the lobby and took the bag from Des as we walked out to his SUV.

Will was headed toward his place. He still lived over the gym, in the apartment that he and Heath had once shared. *I'd Come For You* by Nickelback was playing softly through the sound system. Heath and Lucy were probably staying there since they'd come down for the wedding so I wasn't sure there was room for all of us, but I couldn't think about it too hard. I put my head back, closing my eyes, and listened to the words of the song.

"O, we're here."

My eyes fluttered open and the throbbing in my head started again. I'd fallen asleep on the drive, but recognized the parking lot as I took in my surroundings. Heading up to the apartment, I was surprised to see Heath and Lucy up and about. They both greeted us with hugs and valid concern.

"What time is it?"

"It's eight. You guys need to get some rest." It was later in the morning than I thought. Lucy's statement was directed toward both of us, but her eyes were on Des. She took Des' hand, "Come on. I already changed the sheets." Walking us into her bedroom, Lucy added, "Heath and I are headed back up north, but if you guys need anything, please don't hesitate. You're welcome to stay here as long as you need." Des just nodded, surprised by the generosity, but I wasn't. Lucy walked over to me and rubbed my arm, "You guys are welcome at the lake house anytime. We'd love to have you." Lowering her voice, "I really like her, O, but she's been through a lot. Go easy on her. Tread lightly, love persistently, and be strong. She's going to push you away. Don't let her."

Lucy left the room, closing the door behind her. Des had walked into the attached bathroom and I gave her the privacy I was sure she wanted. Staring at the bed, the exhaustion hit me like a punch to the gut. Kicking off my shoes before dropping my pants, I pulled back the covers and lowered myself to the bed. Removing my prosthetic and rubbing my leg, after the discomfort began to ease, I laid down.

~ ODYSSEUS ~

~ CHAPTER 11 ~

I woke to the sounds of mumbling and soon realized it was Des in the throes of a nightmare. Softly, I tried talking to her to soothe her. It was when she started whimpering in her sleep and crying out, that my compassion and anger came head to head. This was Saul's doing and that S.O.B. was still out there. Even in her dreams she was running from him.

"No!"

I closed the space between our bodies and ran my hand down her arm. She wasn't facing me, but when I leaned over her I saw the tears pooling on her cheek. "Shh, Des, you're ok. You're safe." She began to flail out and sat upright, panting. I tried reassuring her, "You're safe, Des."

Her eyes met mine as I leaned up on my elbow; she was still sobbing, and her words hit me hard, "I'll never be safe, not until he's dead."

"Des, that's not true." Part of it was probably true, but I couldn't say that to her. I wanted him dead, too, but I wasn't willing to sacrifice my life with her to go to prison for the rest of it. Self-defense was another topic all together. I couldn't just murder him in cold blood. "I'll do anything in my power to protect you and so will my brothers. You're one of us now and we're not going to let anything happen to you."

She didn't say anything, just pushed me down to my back and curled into my side. Trembling, she clung to me almost as tightly as I did her. The pounding in my head began to subside as sleep claimed her and it wasn't long before I was sleeping too.

I woke to Des on her cell phone. She was calling work and rescheduling her patients for the next couple days. I needed to do the same thing and turned to sit on the side of the bed. Reaching for my prosthetic, I put it on, and then stood.

"I'm sorry. Did I wake you?"

"It's ok. I need to get up. I need to get someone to cover my clients for the week. Do you know if Will is still here?"

"I'm not sure. I haven't left the room yet." Something was bothering her and then she asked, "Can we go to your place? I don't have anything here."

"Let me see if Will's here. He was supposed to grab some things."

"Ok. I can call the detective. I don't even know if we're allowed in there."

I walked out of the bedroom and she followed. Will wasn't anywhere to be found, but there was a note on the counter. He was down at the gym and had sent one of his trainers over to Montrose to cover my clients there. He was always on top of things.

After speaking to the detective, we were given permission to go to the apartment. He even said he'd send someone to meet us so that we felt safe. Walking into the apartment, her face grew pale. I gave her hand a comforting squeeze as we walked further inside. She stopped moving and I followed her line of sight. Staring into the closet, where she'd hidden before Saul attacked us both, I saw the fear wash over her.

"We don't have to do this, Des."

She just shook her head and inhaled deeply. "No, it's fine."

She headed toward the bedroom and headed for the closet. Pulling out a duffel bag, she set it on the shredded mattress and then opened the drawers holding her clothes. As she pulled her intimates out, we discovered that ninety percent of them had been destroyed. Scissors or a knife had turned them all into useless scraps. Most of her wardrobe was found the same way. As it all sank in I was becoming more infuriated at the thought of how long Saul had been in our place. He hadn't touched a single item of my clothing.

"We'll get you new stuff, Des." She just nodded.

Grabbing some boxes, we threw all the ruined items in and the few items that were still in one piece she threw in the duffel bag. I picked up a scrap of denim and placed it in the box.

"Hey! That's my skirt."

She snatched it from the box and held it up in front of her and I recognized *that* skirt. It was the same skirt—if you could call it that—she wore the night she asked me to meet her at O'Grady's. I couldn't deny the reaction my cock had at the sight of her in that skirt. She had legs for days and that 'skirt' just accentuated them.

"You call *that* a skirt? Does it even cover your ass?"

Pursing her lips, a slight smile formed as she said, "Barely. Maybe I'll show you sometime."

"Mmm." She didn't miss me adjusting myself as I went back to packing our bags.

"I can't believe we now have two apartments that we're paying for that we're not living in." She dropped to the bed in a huff. "What are we going to do, O?"

I sat down next to her and she dropped her head to my shoulder. "I don't know. We'll figure it out. Will won't throw us out, but it's not the ideal situation."

It was a whisper when she asked, "What if he finds us there, too?"

It'd already crossed my mind and when I was on the phone with the detective he'd let me know that squad cars would be sitting outside the gym 24/7 until they found Saul. While I know that should've made me feel safe, it didn't. Saul had already proven he was smart enough to get to us.

The next couple of weeks passed with no word on Saul. He'd stopped showing up to work, of course that'd happened after he assaulted Des at her place. We still had a patrol car at Will's place 24/7, but we didn't even know if Saul was dead or alive. I had to believe that if he was dead we'd have known.

Des decided to put her apartment on the market and was also considering subletting it. Her biggest concern was for the safety of anyone who may want it. I did the same with mine. We agreed that staying with Will was the best bet for now and we'd find a new place together when both places were sold—knowing Saul was our biggest concern. We wanted a place of our own, but also wanted to know we were safe.

My apartment had been cleaned out with the help of my brothers and sold quicker than we expected. One down, one to go. Des still had a shadow of fear that crossed her face on occasion. She didn't talk about it much, but it was lessening. The doctors had cleared me from my concussion and my leg was almost back to feeling normal.

The craving I was beginning to have for her was palpitating. I knew I couldn't push her and slowly her defenses were coming back down, but I was growing desperate for her. She was in the bathroom getting ready for the day when I stepped out of the shower. Sitting down in the chair where my prosthetic sat, I dried my leg before pulling some boxer briefs to mid-thigh, then put my leg back on. Standing, my erection taunted me at half-mast. My eyes caught hers as she looked at my reflection in the mirror, blatantly staring at my crotch.

"See something you like?" Her eyes darted up as she went back to putting on her makeup. She ignored my comment and didn't say a word. Walking up behind her, I kissed the side of her neck. "I miss you." I felt her body relax as I pulled her hair aside and continued kissing her neck.

Her breathing picked up as she leaned into me. My hands circled her waist and fingered the hem of her shirt, her warm silky skin awaiting my touch. I had to leave her wanting more, it was the only way.

Stepping away from her, I warned, "You're going to be late for work." I walked back to the bedroom and got dressed.

~ ODYSSEUS ~

~ CHAPTER 12 ~

I got home that night to a candlelit dinner waiting for me. Music played and the aroma of something Italian filled my senses. I was ravenous. I didn't see her anywhere, but I could smell her perfume. Perfume she hadn't worn since the wedding.

"Des?"

"Sit down. I'll be right there."

"Where's Will?" I shouted from the table.

"Don't worry. I got rid of him for the night." She popped her head around the bedroom door. "He's staying with Dorian and D tonight." Before I could inquire more, she stepped into the room and stole my breath.

She wore that scrap of a mini skirt, black strappy heels and a flowy top. I didn't know where to look first. Her hair fell down her back and her makeup had been touched up. I could tell by the way her lips glistened.

"Shit." She smiled and then became nervous. "You look, just, wow."

"Thank you." She smiled coyly and then walked to the kitchen and pulled a dish out of the oven. Carrying it to the table, she set it down and then went back to the kitchen. "I hope you like lasagna."

"Seriously? Who doesn't? This looks and smells amazing."

When she set the salad down next to me, I pulled her to my lap. She didn't resist me and I was so grateful for it. Instead, she leaned in and kissed my cheek. "I don't want to be apart any longer, O."

Breathe by Ryan Star started playing as she started to say more and I stopped her. "You don't have to explain." Cupping her cheek, my fingers caressing the sensitive skin behind her ear I asked, "Tell me I can kiss you, Des."

"Please kiss me, O. I want you to kiss me, need you to..."

My mouth covered hers as she moaned, surrendering to my kiss. God how I missed kissing her. She kissed like no one else and I couldn't get enough of her satin lips and velvet tongue. Her lip gloss tasted like candy as I greedily pulled her bottom lip between my teeth, licking it clean. One hand circled her back as the other moved down to her leg. Pulling her closer, her legs wedged between mine as she sat on my thigh. My cock throbbed and as she tried to get closer to me, her leg brushing against me caused my erection to leap.

Groaning, she stilled before running her hand down my side. Her fingers played with the elastic of my gym shorts as she confessed, "I want you inside me, O."

Opening my eyes, I stared back into hers and listened to the lyrics of the song. I wanted all her cares and concerns to be gone, given to me to deal with. All I wanted for her was happiness and pleasure and I wanted to be the one to give them to her. She was so full of life when I finally met her that day at therapy and I wanted *that* Des back.

Admittedly, I'd had my eye on her for a while, in awe of her beauty and grace. I was so nervous that day and almost walked out, the nerves getting to me. What I hadn't expected were the sparks between us to be so potent. It was the best surprise, even though she tried fighting it.

"I want that too." I kissed her softly and then pushed her off my lap. "Eat." Her brow scrunched up as I chuckled. "There's no rush. Let's eat." I yanked her closer as she stood and buried my face in her belly, my hand roaming up the back of her leg, almost touching her ass. "I promise, after we eat."

When she stepped back, the glaze in her eyes gave her away, though she didn't know it. I wanted her a complete puddle of want when I took her. It was what she needed and what I craved. There couldn't be any doubt or worry about what we were about to do when we finally consummated our marriage. There were too many demons in both our closets threatening to wreak havoc on our relationship. If I wanted her crying out for more, foreplay and anticipation would be key.

She scooped some lasagna onto our plates and I moved closer to her. Eating with one hand, the other ran up and down her leg the entire time we ate. Soon, she reached out and placed her hand on my neck, her fingers digging into the tight flesh of my neck and shoulders.

I helped her clear the plates and put the leftovers in the fridge. When we were done, she took my hand and led me to the bedroom. I pushed my own nerves down knowing far too well how long it'd been since I'd made love to a woman, having tried and failed on a couple of occasions since my injury.

Walking into the room, she turned to face me and pulled the shirt over her head. A black bra covered her perfect breasts and my hands reached for her without delay. Feeling her skin under my hands was everything I remembered. Her hands ran under my shirt and over my torso. Pulling the shirt up my sides, I helped her remove it from my body.

"I hope you don't mind if I put some music on." I shook my head. "All I think about when I hear this song is you."

"Let's hear it."

She pushed some buttons on her phone, set in on the dresser and informed me of the song. "It's *Beautiful With You* by Halestorm. And it's on repeat." Smiling, she looked me over and sighed softly, "You've been working out. Hard."

One side of my mouth turned up as I confirmed, "Yes. All about the gains." She chuckled as I added, "Been a little frustrated. Working out helps."

"I'm sorry I've been so distant."

"Don't ever apologize for that, Des. I'm not going anywhere." Bending my face toward hers, hands gripped my lower back as our mouths met. "Tell me to stop and know that I will." She just nodded and continued kissing me.

I tangled my hands in her hair, holding her face to mine. Her own sank into the back of my shorts and gripped my ass before she pulled the shorts down. They puddled at the floor as her fingers ran up and down my hips, my cock desperate for her touch. My hands moved down to trace over the top of her breasts, then pulled the bra straps down.

Turning her, I unclasped her bra as I nipped and sucked on her neck. As the bra fell from her body, I cupped her breasts and kneaded them as she sank back against me, the top of her ass rubbing against my dick.

"O, don't stop."

My hands ran over her belly and to the snap closure of her skirt. Tugging it open before I pushed it down her thighs, black lace panties I hadn't seen before met my fingers. Moving my hands down her ass, to her thighs, and around to pull her hips back against me.

"Touch me, O."

I dipped my hand between her legs and found her panties already soaked through. "I want to taste you, Des. Please tell me I can taste you."

A shudder ran through her as she turned to face me. "You can taste me, please taste me."

Kissing me, her tongue collided with mine and she didn't stop till we were both breathless. With us both only in our underwear, I walked to the bed and sat down against the headboard, motioning her to climb up in front of me. Placing a foot on each side of my hips, she stared down at me as I slowly ran my thumb over her lace covered mound. Her eyes closed and her hips pushed a little closer as I put a little more pressure on her clit.

"Odysseus…" It was barely a whisper and I wasn't even sure if she knew she'd said it.

Slipping my thumbs under her panties, I pulled them down and helped her step out of them. I was salivating at the thought of her in my mouth and dripping down my chin and her scent just accentuated it. I looked up to her, the glaze heavy over her eyes, and leaned in to kiss her hips. Her hand came down on my head as she gently tugged on my hair. Cupping her ass, I pulled her close as my tongue slid along her lips.

She tasted like redemption, like a sweet tart I'd never get enough of, and I knew it after just one taste. Her soft moans began to fill the room as her hips began to rock against my face. Slipping my hand between her thighs, I slid a finger inside her as she pulsed around it.

"O, please…Oh, God."

My lips circled around her clit as I sucked on it gently, my tongue softly stroking it. It wasn't long before I felt her ass clench in my hands.

She was close and I felt like a God when she came in my mouth. She chanted my name and I thought she might pull the hair from the roots, she was gripping my scalp so tight.

I pulled her down into my lap and she collapsed against my chest, straddling me. I traced my hands over every inch of her flesh until the tremors subsided. She lifted her head, a silly grin on her face and then she kissed me. Rubbing against my erection, she planted herself against me. The warmth of her against me had my cock thrumming with need.

"Make love to me, O."

She continued kissing me and then reached for the night stand. Pulling out a box of condoms, she climbed off my lap and sat on the edge of the bed as she opened it. Moving to the edge, she didn't miss a beat. She knelt in front of me, massaging my thighs before pulling the boxer briefs from my hips. She'd torn a single foil packet off and set it down next to us.

I grabbed the wrapped condom, anxiety beginning to flood me. My eyes stared at my prosthetic and my hands began to shake. I could do this, I wanted this, and I wanted her. We'd been married for almost a month and had yet to consummate, thanks to Saul. Her hand came down on my shoulder, sending my thoughts scattering.

"Odysseus?"

I loved hearing my given name falling from her lips. We were both naked and I began wondering what was wrong with me. Why wasn't I pouncing on her, sinking my dick into her, the place I wanted it most? I sucked in a sharp breath as her hands began running up my thighs again. She'd been more than accepting of my injury and was somewhat immune to it considering her line of work.

"Do you want to take it off?" I looked to it and back to her and nodded once. Setting the condom back down, I reached for my leg and she stopped me, "I can do it."

Once she removed the prosthetic and the dressings, she began running her hands over the sensitive skin. I felt myself relax again under her touch as her hands slowly began moving upward. Our eyes locked as she began massaging my dick and he sprang back to life, harder than ever. Running a hand through her long hair, I leaned down to kiss her. It was a slow kiss full of nips and lip tugging before her tongue reached out to mine.

Reaching under her arms, I pulled her up to stand between my legs. Releasing my cock from her grip, he didn't budge, jutting out between us. I ran my hands over her soft, yet toned, stomach and around to her ass. Drifting down the seam of her crack, I didn't stop until the dampness on her inner thighs met my hands. Pulling gently, she parted her legs as her arousal filled my senses.

I looked up and found her eyes closed, head dropped to the side as she steadied herself on my shoulder with one hand. Looking to her sex, I ran my fingers back and forth over her lips as they parted for me, her wetness coating my fingers. I circled her clit as a moan escaped her and her fingers clenched on my shoulder. After a moment, I dipped my middle finger inside her as we groaned in unison.

"O, please don't make me beg."

Sliding my fingers out of her, I pulled her closer and she bent down until we were nose to nose, my cock wedged between us. Before I knew it, she had the condom wrapper in her hand before opening it and discarding it. She slid the cool latex down my length expertly, fondling my balls when she was done. On her knees, she wrapped her arms around my neck and settled her warmth against my own.

"Show me how much you want me, O."

She'd been patient with me tonight as the tension built. Now my insecurities were the only thing standing in our way. Now it was my chance to prove how much I wanted her.

Positioning myself at her opening, I slid the tip in. "I want you, Des."

"How much?" She molded her mouth to mine as we kissed deeply.

Gripping her hips, I slammed her down on me as we moaned. "This much." She panted in my mouth as we exchanged the air we breathed and she pulsed around me. "Show me you want me, too."

With our lips joined, she slid up and down my cock as her breasts rubbed against my chest. Lost in the sensations, she pulled back letting her hair cascade down her back. Unable to resist, I pulled on it causing her breasts to thrust higher in the air. Suckling on them in turn, I moved my hand between us and caressed her clit as she rode me.

I wanted nothing more than for her to come again. It was a primal need I had as a man. Knowing I could satisfy her sexually was a better high than my own orgasm would ever be. I scooted further onto the bed and she pushed me to my back. Fiercely, her arms clung around my shoulders as her hips grinded against mine.

"O, you feel so good."

"I want you to come."

Leaning up, she looked in my eyes and I noticed they were a darker shade of blue, appearing heavy with lust, that glaze of hers. "Come with me."

Grinning, "Don't wait on my account." Don't get me wrong. I wanted to come, but I could hold off a few more minutes considering she seemed to already be headed to her peak once more.

Her tits bounced as I held her hips, though she was doing all the work. "O, I'm close." Her movement became more frantic as she made one last request. "Kiss me Odysseus, kiss me as I come."

Reaching up, I cupped her face as she began to shake. Pulling her face down to mine, I kissed her as she came. She always had the same request and now was the time to fulfill it. Her body convulsed against mine, her kiss distracted and passionate all at once. Her movements eventually slowed as her kiss became more focused. I was still rock hard, but knew she would be sensitive, maybe too sensitive. Her hands ran over my sides as my dick pulsed inside her.

"Thank you."

"You don't have to thank me."

She sat up and moved around me gently, causing my hips to buck. "O, we're not leaving this bed until you get off, too."

Smirking, I grabbed hold of her and flipped her to her back and pushed into her again. "Is that what you want?"

Her eyes rolled back as she panted, "That's pretty good." Her hands grabbed my ass as I found her ankle and placed it on my shoulder. "Oh, better." Her other foot ran down the muscles of my good leg as I pumped in and out of her. "Fuck, O!"

And that's what I did. My body spent over a year fighting a battle only my head and heart could win. With her help, in that moment, I felt whole again, like nothing about me was different. "Desiree! Fuck."

"It's ok, O. Take it, take me. Whatever you need." She met every thrust and began crying out like she might come again, but I couldn't stop myself. My orgasm was now inevitable.

"Des..." I dropped fully onto her as I filled the condom. I didn't think it would ever stop, my hips continuing to buck into her as she kissed and cooed against my neck. When the sensations finally stopped I was overcome with emotion and rolled away.

What the fuck was wrong with me? "Hey, you ok?" She curled around my back and asked if she did something wrong. "I'm sorry, did I do something wrong?"

I couldn't stand the self-doubt in her voice and croaked out, "It's not you."

"O," she forced me to look at her and I was ashamed and embarrassed. She took in the tears in my eyes and she seemed to understand. She was way too intuitive, a similar complaint she had about me. "Was this, I mean, have you not had sex since your injury?"

I shook my head. I hadn't had sex with a woman since the desert and I hadn't realized how much of a toll it'd taken on me. Scared and worried of never being accepted again, I'd hid behind a façade of pride and confidence. I couldn't even get it up that night with Stacey, when I was supposed to be with Des. "I should've told you."

Laying on my chest, she pulled my arms around her as she agreed, "Yes, you should've. But everything else makes so much more sense now." Stroking my stomach she continued, "It's a big deal. Your first time after an injury like that. I hope it was as good for you as it was for me."

Tilting her chin, I locked my eyes to hers and pleaded with her soul. "It was amazing. Don't doubt that. I'm sorry I didn't tell you, but I wouldn't change a thing." I kissed her, rolling to my side so we were chest to chest. Running my nose along hers I whispered, "Thank you, Des. I don't know how to thank you enough."

Giggling, she took my hand and placed it over her mound. "You can do it again."

Smiling against her mouth, I encouraged her, "I think I like this side of you."

~ ODYSSEUS ~

~ CHAPTER 13 ~

I woke up to find her sprawled on her stomach next to me. Her hair that was a mixture of browns and golds fanned out across the pillow. Her lips were slightly parted as she breathed softly. I loved watching her sleep. That night at her apartment when she fell asleep in my lap was when I knew I was in big trouble with her. She was stunning and while she used the façade of an ego to match her beauty, she really didn't have one. Behind the beautiful outer shell was just another insecure girl, looking for someone to convince her she was worth more than she thought she was.

She had no idea how much she was worth to me and I had a feeling I'd never be able to convince her of that. My hands drifted to her hair as I began running my fingers through the silky strands. She mumbled my name and crawled back into my arms where she stayed the rest of the night.

Over the next few weeks, tension rose and fell. Saul was still on the loose and it was taking its toll on all of us.

"I just want to do things that normal couples do. I want to go to the movies and out to dinner without having to look over my shoulder." I understood how she felt because I wanted the same thing.

"I know you do. I'm sorry, Des." We were staring at each other over the kitchen island when Will walked in.

He was chugging down a bottle of water and it was clear he'd just finished working out. "Hey. What's for dinner, Des?"

She rolled her eyes and bit out, "Screw you, Will. What do I look like?"

I chuckled at the way they'd grown comfortable around one another. Will loved to give Lucy a hard time and since she wasn't around anymore, Des filled those shoes. One of these days he was going to get a 'what for' from all these women. That, or karma would get him one way or another. It was going to take one special lady to deal with him. There was a great guy in there, he was just hiding behind years of loneliness and hurt.

"That lasagna was killer. What do I need to do to get you to make more?"

"Nothing. I only make my *special* lasagna for the man who eats my pussy and that's not you." Will started choking on his water and I would've too had I been drinking any. She smirked, knowing she'd caught him off guard. "Any other requests?"

"Hot damn, O. Got yourself a live one there."

I nodded and said, "Yes, yes I do." I looked to my wife who was quite pleased with herself and then asked, "How about we order takeout? Italian does sound good!"

"Yes. I'm game. Their lasagna's better anyways." He was goading her and I just waited for her retort.

"Maybe so. But," she looked directly at my cock and then smiled at me before looking to Will, "I'm in the mood for sausage and I hear you're fresh out."

"Alright. That's enough." I pushed Will into his room before they took the bantering too far. "Go shower, I'll order dinner."

"He learned all his best moves from me, Des. Let me know when you tire of him."

"Hey!" Will shrugged his shoulders and grinned. "Too far man. Knock it off."

"She started it." He slammed the door before I could respond. Turning back toward Des, I found her nearly in stitches. "What's so funny? I don't mind you bantering with my brother, but that was a little too much." I heard the door open behind me as Will snapped a towel at me. I immediately covered my dick and bellowed at him, "You're an asshole." Looking to Des, who was now holding her belly, "And you. This calls for punishment."

"Oh, I'm scared! What are you going to do to me, Odysseus?" She narrowed her eyes at me, lips pouting as she wiped under her eyes. Tears had leaked from her laughing so hard.

"You'll just have to wait and see." I continued grumbling as I pulled out the takeout menus from a drawer in the island.

Her arms twisted around my waist, "You're not really mad are you? We were just messing with you."

"Flirting with my brother." I turned and stared down at her as she ran her hand over my crotch. "That makes it better."

Softly, she cooed, "I bet it does." Her hand palmed me as she squeezed lightly and then got up on her tiptoes to kiss me. "Want me to suck it, O?" She began kissing my neck as she continued stroking me. "I want to suck you off while you return the favor."

Groaning, "Sixty-nine, huh. I might be up for that."

"I dealt with enough of this shit with Heath and Lucy. Take it to your room." She kissed me once more and then walked away as I adjusted myself. "Fuck. I'm not flaunting ladies around here. Show some respect."

"You'd have to have ladies first, Will." She pulled three beers out of the fridge and handed Will one and he mock laughed at her. "I've got some single friends. One of them might be willing to do a pity lay."

"Uncle! I give up. You win." I started drinking the beer she handed me as we laughed at Will. He glared at me, "Fuck, dude. She fits right in. Maybe too well."

"Yes, yes she does."

"You can thank med school. You wouldn't believe the crap we chicks deal with. You either fight back or learn to take it."

Sarcastically, Will confirmed, "Clearly you decided to just take it."

"You know it."

After dinner we were cuddled on the couch; Will had long since left to meet Dorian and D at the bar. My cell rang and she begged me not to answer it. Ignoring her plea, I saw that it was Will and hesitantly answered. Was he drunk dialing me?

"What's up, Will? What?" I continued to listen and then my call waiting went off. "Hang on, Will." Looking to my phone I recognized the number of the detective. "Shit," Des sat up, concern all over her face as I walked a few steps away from her. Switching over I said, "This is O."

"O, we've spotted him. Are you both home?"

"Yes."

"Stay there. He vandalized your brother's car at the bar and was spotted a few blocks from your place."

"Listen to me. You find him. This has gone on long enough. Keep me posted when you have some real information." Switching the call back over to Will, I asked, "Do you need a ride? Ok. I'll come and get you."

I slid the phone into my pocket and noticed Des was curled up in a ball on the couch. Sitting down next to her, I placed my hand on her back.

"What'd he do?"

"He vandalized Will's SUV and confronted him in the bar. By the time Will realized who he was, he took off."

She was shaking her head, "Why is he doing this, why would he confront Will?" Her hands covered her face as I tucked her in against me. Pushing me off of her, "This is my fault. He won't stop until he has me."

Gripping her shoulders, I barked, "He's not getting you. Over my dead body."

Crying out, "That's what I'm afraid of! He's already shot you once." Tears fell from her eyes and this time when I reached for her, she climbed into my lap and wrapped her arms and legs around me. "I love you so much."

Stroking her hair and holding her tight I tried to soothe her. "I love you, too. Nothing's going to happen to me. Promise."

"I wish that was a promise you could keep."

Her somber words irked me. Saul had her convinced that if he wanted to get to her, eventually he would. I couldn't blame her. The cops had done a shit job at protecting her. But if that motherfucker thought I'd lay down and take it, he had another thing coming. I'd been to war before. This was a cake walk in comparison...except that the person I was protecting this time was more precious to me than any other before.

"Stay here. Don't open the door for anyone." She bolted her head back and gawked at me. "I have to go get Will."

"I'm not staying here alone. I'm coming with you."

"The patrol car is downstairs, Des..."

"NO! I'm coming with you. Or send the patrol car for Will."

Sighing, I knew it was pointless to argue with her. "Alright. Come on."

~ ODYSSEUS ~

~ CHAPTER 14 ~

We hopped in my truck and headed toward the bar Will had said he was at. She stared out the passenger window as I kept checking the rearview mirror. I had a bad feeling and was starting to regret not staying home and sending someone else to get Will. But he was there alone, Dorian and D having already left with women and they weren't answering their phones.

We pulled into the parking lot and I spotted Will toward the back talking to a tow truck driver. That was fast. We both hopped out of my truck, when I spotted the patrol car pull in behind us. I wouldn't miss the constant tail when this was all over. Stepping over to Will's SUV, I was heartbroken. It'd been a beautiful SUV and now the windows were smashed and all four tires slashed.

"Jesus, dude. I'm sorry."

He shrugged his shoulders, "That's what insurance is for. Real winner you picked there, Des." Will was trying to lighten the mood, but I knew it wouldn't.

"Fuck you. Cuz this was part of my grand plan, to have him go after everyone I know and love." She stormed off and I gave Will a dirty look before following after her.

"Des, wait."

All hell broke loose. The sound of a gun firing had me leaping on top of her, taking her down to the gravel. I was aware of some shouting and then more gun fire. Crawling behind another vehicle, I sheltered her with my body.

"Are you ok?"

"Yes, I think so. You?"

I was already attempting to check my surroundings when another shot whizzed over my head. "God dammit." I positioned her behind the tire for the most protection and spotted Will. He'd seen something, someone, and was going after him. "Will!" He ignored me as I cursed. "Shit!"

The deputy made his way to us and started talking on his radio. More units were headed our way. "Where's your brother?" I pointed to where Will had been. "Shit. He's going after him."

Without another word he took off after Will once he ordered us to stay put. It was becoming too much for me to handle. Memories of the desert were bombarding me as I tried to fight them off. Gripping my head between my hands, I was aware of her trying to calm me.

"O, you're ok. Just breathe, O." Her soft hands cupped my face. "You're getting out of this." Before I could stop her, she stood and began yelling Saul's name. "Saul! SAUL!"

When I managed to get on my feet again, the horror that unfolded nearly paralyzed me. I'd become familiar with his picture and saw him walk toward Des. He was a good twenty to thirty feet away, but it was twenty to thirty feet too close. Where the fuck was Will and the deputy? Saul's eyes were transfixed on Des. I seized the moment and crept along the wall, out of his line of sight.

Des started talking to him and I refused to listen. My leg kicked something and his eyes found me in the shadows. That was when his arm lifted and we all saw the gun. Will was behind him, getting closer as Des pleaded with him.

"He's too young for you, Des, and a cripple. I should put him out of his misery like the dog he is."

"I know, Saul. You're right. But you don't have to kill him. If you kill him we can't be together." I knew she was baiting him, but the words hurt.

"You're lying." He looked to me again, "I'd stop moving motherfucker!"

"HEY!"

It was the distraction I needed. Will started baiting him knowing he couldn't shoot all three of us at the same time. Then I spotted the deputy behind Saul, the four of us forming a circle around Saul. He couldn't take the shot, not with Des standing in front of Saul.

Saul swung the gun back and forth between Will and I then demanded, "Pick one, Des. You're screwing them both, aren't you? You always were a little too promiscuous for my taste." He spit it out again, "PICK ONE!"

Des just shook her head, her eyes locked on mine. "Pick me! Let them be. I'll go with you." She started walking toward Saul.

"Des!"

Will sprung into action before anyone knew what was happening. He and Saul fell to the ground as I made my way closer yelling Will's name. "Will!"

A gun went off and then Will was straddling Saul and began pummeling his face. Will pinned Saul's hand above his head and together we managed to get the gun away from him. Before anyone could stop me, I picked Saul up and began assaulting him.

"Ma'am, put the gun down!"

That got my attention. Turning I found the gun in Des' trembling hands. I wasn't sure where Will was, but I was holding Saul's nearly lifeless body, quickly releasing him after one more blow to the face. I threw him down in front of the deputy and stepped in front of Des.

"Des, look at me."

Shaking her head, the gun still aimed at Saul, the deputy ordered her to lower the gun once more.

"We got him. You're safe now."

"No, we won't be safe until he's dead. He won't stop."

I couldn't let her do this. He was defenseless at the moment. "Des, we got him. It's over." It was then that Will groaned. Des and I looked to him as he pulled his hands from his gut. He was covered in blood. "Will!"

"I'm fine." It was dark and I wasn't sure if he was fine or not.

"See. He won't stop."

I took a step closer and grabbed her wrist. "Drop it, Des. Now!" She let go of her hold and I threw the gun aside. The deputy cuffed Saul as I gathered her to my side. "It's over."

"Shit." My attention back on Will, we rushed to his side as other deputies pulled up. "Fuck, I don't think I'm fine."

"Jesus Christ, Will. What did you do?" Des started applying pressure to his abdomen as I screamed for help.

"Hey, O." I returned my eyes to his. "If anything happens to me..."

"Nothing's going to happen to you." He groaned and dropped his head back. "Will, you fight this. You're going to be fine."

Des had silent tears rolling down her cheeks as she kept the pressure on his wound. When the paramedics arrived, she started talking all medical, and then they took over. Immediately they loaded him on a gurney and into the back of the ambulance. A deputy offered to drive us to the hospital and we agreed.

When we got to the hospital they'd already taken Will up for emergency surgery. Des got us cleaned up and began calling everyone. Not only had I not protected Des, I hadn't protected Will. I punched the wall and immediately regretted it.

"O!" Des grabbed my hand and examined my bloody knuckles. "You trying to break your hand?"

She sat me down and I dropped my head pulling my hand from hers. Rubbing my back, she placed her head on my shoulder. We sat that way until our family started arriving. Dorian came barreling through the doors, intimidating everyone in his path. He was a big dude and mean to boot. Not really mean, but it was very hard to penetrate his defenses. That was a story for another day.

"What the fuck happened? How is he?" Des started talking and he cut her off. "I asked my brother, not you."

"Dorian, this isn't her fault."

"Isn't it?"

Des stood up after kissing my cheek. "It's ok. I'll give you a few minutes."

As she walked away, my parents walked in and my mom immediately wrapped her arms around Des. She pointed to where Dorian and I were and my parents headed over. D ran in the door a few minutes later. We sat for at least another hour still waiting for news.

~ ODYSSEUS ~

~ CHAPTER 15 ~

Des was sitting on the other side of the waiting room when her cell rang. She answered it and spoke quietly into the phone. When she was finished with the call she walked over, like she was worried she was interrupting. My mother moved over and motioned Des to sit down between us.

"That was Lucy. They're almost here."

I grabbed her hand right as two doctors emerged from the back hallway. Pulling masks from their faces, they made their way over to us. My parents stood and we all followed suit. The doctors told us to sit back down and joined us.

"He made it through." We all exhaled the breaths we were holding and Des squeezed my hand. "It was touch and go for a while, but he should make a full recovery." I didn't hear anything else the doctors said. Will was going to be fine and that was what mattered.

The mood was lighter and we sat and waited till we could go visit Will. He was in recovery and we had to wait for him to be moved to a room. Needing fresh air, I took a walk outside to help pass the time. I hadn't realized she'd followed me until I heard Lucy and Heath call our names.

Lucy hugged Des and looked her over before making her way to me. "Is there any word yet?"

"He made it. Doctors are confident he'll make a full recovery."

You could almost see the relief roll off of Heath and Lucy, especially Heath. She clung to Heath and wiped a tear from his eye when she pulled away. We were all brothers and our bond was strong, but the bond Heath and Will had was different, stronger, as it should be with twins.

A few hours later Des and I walked into his room. He was barely awake and smiled at us, trying to sit up I chastised him. "Lay the fuck down, Will."

Groaning, he dropped his head back against the pillow. "You two ok?"

"We're fine. What you did..." Des couldn't finish her thought and I squeezed her hand.

"You're family now. We protect our own." Will looked to me and asked, "Can I talk to Des, alone?" I nodded and left the room.

Closing the door, I leaned against the wall for several minutes. When laughter started filling my ears, I couldn't wait any longer and barged back through the doors. Des was sitting at the foot of his bed and smiling. Will looked like the cat who'd caught the canary.

"Should I be concerned?" Glaring at Will, "I know how you like to steal your brothers' women."

Des balked and Will glared at me. "I haven't stolen anyone. I can't help if it bitches find me irresistible."

I shook my head as Des climbed off the bed and made her way over to me. "We were just talking, about you to be specific. He's not competition for you." She kissed me as Will taunted us.

"I fucking heard that. I'm great competition." Wincing, we looked at him as he clutched his side. "Fuck...that hurts."

"You should get some sleep, Will. You've been through a lot." Des' words echoed my thoughts. She walked over to him and hugged him. "I'll never forget what you did for us, for me, tonight. Thank you."

He hugged her unenthusiastically, like she had cooties, grumbling, "Yeah, yeah. It's nothing." Des stood by the door and I walked to Will's bedside. We clasped hands, our Kerrigan brother handshake never forgotten. He just nodded and grinned, "Go take your wife home and enjoy the privacy. I think I'll be here a day or two."

"Thank you again. I can never repay you."

"You don't need to repay me. Just enjoy your life, and her." He lowered his gaze and for a moment I realized that he was envious of what I had with Des. Not that he wanted her, just wanted what we had, and I wanted that for him, too. "There was no way I was going to let him shoot you or her. You've got something amazing with her and I had to stop that psycho before he hurt one of you."

"Love you, man."

"Love you, too bro."

I woke from a horrible nightmare. As I lay panting and recalling it, I wiped the sweat from my brow. I was in the desert, but so was Des and Saul was there too. He was holding a gun to her head and she was holding something in her arms, but I couldn't make it out. She moaned softly next to me and I pushed the nightmare away.

Our sleep schedules were completely out of whack. I rolled over in bed to see that it was past six p.m. Des slept silently beside me in her racerback pajama shirt and short set. We were finally free of Saul and I prayed he'd spend eternity rotting in jail. How many times had I almost lost Des because of him? I couldn't keep track.

Leaning over her, I rained kisses over her shoulders as I pushed her hair out of the way. My 'morning' wood taunting me. Running my hands down her back and under the covers I discovered she was wearing panties and not the sleep shorts. She moaned softly and lifted her hips. The weight of my body was against her back as I licked and nipped at her neck. Goosebumps covered her flesh as my hand ran over the back of her thighs.

"Des." I rubbed my cock against her hip and she moved closer.

"O, please." She turned to look at me and smiled, "Show me your O face."

Grinning like a fool, I lowered my mouth to hers as my hands continued roaming over her body. Cupping her through her panties, she arched her back and pressed back against my hand. Sitting up, I pulled the scrap of lace down her legs and threw them to the floor. I began kneading and kissing her ass cheeks as she buried her head in the pillow. Spreading her legs a little further apart, her pussy shone back at me. Burying my face between her legs, her body tensed as my tongue licked at her.

Pushing her hips up, her ass rose in the air as her chest and face pressed into the bed. I continued to eat her from behind, my cock eager for attention, as she gently rocked back and forth. My hands ran up and down her sides, from her hips to her ribcage, and I noticed her gripping the headboard.

"O, please. I need more, need you."

I loved looking at her this way. All precautions thrown to the side as we solely focused on the physical. Sitting up between her legs, her pussy inches away from my face, I removed my underwear, and then I slid a finger inside hooking it down to tease her g-spot.

"Ohhh." She stilled before a small shudder ran through her. "That. Right there. Don't stop." She was panting as I stroked my cock with my free hand.

Having to stop myself, I resumed touching the sensitive flesh of her ass and lower back while I pumped my finger in and out of her. Adding a second finger, she moaned even louder. She clenched around me and I could feel her body tense over and over. She was close.

"You're so beautiful. Come for me, Des. I got you."

A few moments later, she fell apart in the most exquisite way. The aftershocks still running through her, I pulled her back to me, her back against my chest. Turning her face to mine I found tears running down her cheeks.

"Des?"

Her hand reached underneath her and found my cock. Lifting slightly, she guided him home. "Take me, O." Her eyes met mine and whispered, "They're happy tears. Remind me whose I am."

Groaning as she lifted and then slid me in further, I panted, "You're mine. Always mine. Only mine."

~ ODYSSEUS ~

~ CHAPTER 16 ~

Circling my arms around her, my hand moved to her mound as she dropped her head to my shoulder. I caressed her breasts through her sleep shirt which she quickly pulled over her head. Entirely naked and fused as one, our bodies claimed one another.

"I'm not wearing a condom, Des."

"I don't care. I just want you, all of you."

I didn't care either. "You have all of me."

My fingers began to move over her clit as she circled her hips, shifting up and down. Leaning forward, she rocked against me and we both moaned at the position. I continued to fuck her, my fingers rubbing her clit while my other hand gathered her hair and pulled.

Gasping, "Don't stop. Oh, God. I'm going to come again, O."

I pulled her back to me and released her hair. Gripping her neck, she turned her mouth to mine, my tongue diving inside. Her cries were muffled as she went stiff in my arms. Her hands were fondling her breasts while I pulled every last tremor from her. I pushed up into her one last time before pushing her forward, never disconnecting our bodies.

I took her hand and placed it over her clit, "Don't stop touching yourself." She just nodded as I pulled all the way out and slid back in, my hand braced against the center of her back. "Is this ok?" Another nod. "What about this?" My thumb pressed at her back opening as I continued pumping my cock in and out of her. She nodded. "I need to hear you say it, Des."

"It's perfect. Don't stop."

I wasn't sure how much I had left in me, but I was going to fucking enjoy it. She pulled her hand away, sucking on her fingers, before resuming the task I'd given her. She never stopped twitching and tensing around me and sooner than I wanted, I knew I was close. My thumb now fully in her ass, I slowed my pursuit and fisted myself as I rubbed myself all over her lips.

"O! Put it back!"

Smiling, I teased her, "Put what back?" Before she could respond, I slammed back in causing her to groan.

"Oh, shit. I can't come again."

"Yes, you can. Tell me when." I moved my thumb in and out as she screamed.

"Now!"

As she pulsed around me, I held back as long as I could. Removing my thumb, I gripped her hip before falling on top of her. My hips continuing to move as she panted underneath me. My face found hers and kissed her until I had to come up for air.

"I love you, Des."

"I love you." I rolled off of her and pulled her close. "I might not be able to walk, but I love you for it."

"Was that three times?"

"Yes! No need to brag."

"I'm not bragging. Not yet! I'll brag when we exceed three!" I winked at her as she rolled her eyes.

We laid there for a few minutes when she apologized. "I'm really sorry about everything." Her voice broke and I lifted her chin.

"Des, baby. Stop. It's not your fault. He's locked up now. You're safe! I'll always protect you."

"I know. I just. I want to forget everything about him. I just want to have some peace."

"It's coming, starting right now. I promise."

It was now the middle of May. Will had come home after almost a week in the hospital. I think they were happy to get rid of his complaining ass. We still hadn't been able to sell Des' place and she was ecstatic when she finally got an offer—a cash one at that—above asking. They asked that the furnishings stay and she agreed, knowing we wanted our own place and new things we'd pick out together.

"Can we start looking for a place?" She was smiling from ear to ear and I couldn't help but want to tease her.

"I kind of like it here. Don't you want to stay here and take care of me and my brother?" She smacked my shoulder as I surrendered. "I'm kidding, Des."

"I love your brother, but we're newlyweds. I want our *own* place." She leaned into my ear and whispered, "I want to scream at the top of my lungs and let you fuck me on the counter without worrying about someone walking in on us."

My cock twitched as I sucked her ear into my mouth. "I like the sound of that. What did you have in mind?"

"I think a two bedroom is a must, maybe a house..."

"That's not what I meant." She narrowed her eyes at me as I inquired, "You mentioned the counter. Where else do you want me to fuck you?"

Grinning, she said, "Well, I'll know when we find the place!"

Saul was in lockup, waiting for his trial to start. He'd hired a big-time lawyer and was able to drag everything out. Des, Will, and I had all made our statements—numerous times—about what had happened that night and knew we'd be called to testify when the time came.

Des' parents had come for a visit, but only stayed one night. They refused to talk about much of anything having to do with her career and I understood why she'd been anxious to have them visit. Her father was pretty self-absorbed and constantly on his phone. Her mother wouldn't say anything that could possibly conflict with her father's opinion. She was like a Stepford wife. Perfectly displayed and perfectly agreeable. It was absolutely boring.

They'd been kind and welcoming to me, but also made it evident that they weren't happy with how quickly 'things happened'. I couldn't fathom how Des had turned out the way she did, but was grateful for it. I'd take disagreeable with an opinion any day of the week as opposed to compliant and lifeless.

"I'm sorry. I tried to warn you."

Grinning, "Des, it just makes me appreciate you so much more having met them." She dropped her head and giggled. "Could they be any more self-involved?"

Sighing, "Yes, yes they could. They were pretty well behaved."

"Listen, I've been talking to Heath and Lucy." She nodded and I continued, "They've invited us up for Memorial Weekend. I thought..."

"Yes! Please, yes. Let's go."

"They'll be there, too, we wouldn't be alone, and I think everyone else is coming up on Sunday. I thought we could go up on Friday." I so desperately wanted to give her a honeymoon, but with everything going on it just didn't seem to be in the cards. Not anytime soon.

"It's fine! I love Lucy, she's been so welcoming to me. Is it too soon to pack?"

~ ODYSSEUS ~

~ CHAPTER 17 ~

It was the start of Memorial Day weekend and Des and Lucy had made plans to spend the day together, seemingly my birthday forgotten. Des drove up in the morning and I followed late that afternoon. When I walked into my parent's lake house—which was currently Heath and Lucy's home—I could hear the girls laughing. I hadn't seen Heath's car meaning he was probably still at the gym.

"Seriously! That's what I told her, too!" I walked in on them and just stood and observed. Des jumped up and threw her hands around my neck. "You made it!" She kissed me and announced, "Let vacation begin!"

Lucy took a drink of her wine cooler as I chastised them, "Little early to be drinking isn't it?"

Lucy made a dirty face and said, "It's after five and it's Friday! Beers in the fridge." I grunted and headed to the fridge as Des sat back down with Lucy. I had a feeling these two could cause lots of trouble for Heath and I.

Walking back into the living room, I sat down and Des chirped, "We should go out!" Looking to Lucy, "Are there any bars around here? There's got to be somewhere we can. Bowling, dancing, something!"

Lucy giggled and agreed. "That sounds great. We haven't been *out* in ages. There are a couple of dive bars and a bowling alley with glow-bowl."

"I'm not going to glow-bowl." I turned to see Heath standing in the doorway.

Lucy pouted and I looked away to find Des pouting at me. "Please!" Her hand ran up my thigh as she whispered in my ear. "I'll make it up to you! It'll be fun. Let's go."

Groaning I looked back at Heath. Rolling his eyes, he pried Lucy off of him and conceded. "Fine, I'll go. But I don't have to like it."

The girls jumped up and down and ran off to the bedrooms. "Seriously, how did this happen?"

I put my hands up in defense. "I just got here myself. Don't look at me. They were in cahoots before I walked in the door."

An hour later Heath and I were ready to open another beer each when the girls emerged from the master bedroom. Christ on a cracker. They were playing dirty, at least Des was, and I couldn't focus on anything but her. They totally had this planned, I knew it the minute I saw that miniskirt and black heels.

She cozied up to me and I attempted to order her to change and firmly demanded, "You're not going out in that, Des."

Almost choking on her laugh, she confirmed, "Um, yes I am." Softer, for my ears only, she confessed, "I wore it for you. If you're nice I'll let you take it off later."

Lucy asked, "Ready?"

Des perked up, "Yes! Let's go!"

Heath offered to drive so we all climbed into his car. The girls climbed into the back and I took the passenger seat. We went to a local steakhouse for dinner and then headed to the only bowling alley around for miles. There was a bar attached with a dance floor and we hung out in there until the glow-bowling started. The girls had put our names on the list and now we waited.

Every head in the place turned as the girls walked through the bar. I couldn't blame them, but Heath and I both made it very clear with our body language that they were spoken for. One guy came up and shook Heath's hand. Found out that he owned a small car dealership in town and worked out at Heath's gym.

A waitress walked over, eyes all over Heath. Lucy blatantly sat on his lap and ordered a round of Fireball for all of us. Heath and I tried objecting, but Des and Lucy wouldn't hear of it.

"You can bring some water too for these two lightweights." The waitress nodded, smiled at Heath, and then walked away. I swore I heard Lucy threaten the waitress once she'd walked away. "I'll cut a bitch!"

"Oh stop. She was just being friendly." Heath pulled her close and nuzzled her neck.

"She can be friendly elsewhere."

Des jumped up as a song began playing overhead and pulled Lucy to the floor with her. I looked at my brother, who couldn't take his eyes off of Lucy, and warned, "This is going to be a long fucking night."

Turning to me he winked, "They deserve some fun. We can pay them back at home."

This Summer's Gonna Hurt Like A MotherFucker by Maroon 5 was playing and soon more ladies joined Des and Lucy on the floor. The waitress dropped off four waters and four shots of Fireball. Heath paid her, tipped her generously, and averted his eyes back to the dance floor. Once the song was over the girls sat down, giggling and grabbed the shots. Insisting that Heath and I could handle doing one too, we held up our glasses.

I spoke up and toasted to us. "Here's to living like a normal couple."

Des hooded her eyes and smiled as the three of them repeated, "To living like a normal couple!"

Heath was gagging as Lucy and Des pursed their lips. I'd had my share of Fireball, but didn't care for it. Des leaned into my lap and pulled my face to hers. She kissed me possessively, all tongue, and ran her fingernails over the back of my neck.

Seductively, she cooed, "Happy Birthday, baby!" Biting at my earlobe she asked, "Would it be normal to let you fuck me in the bathroom?"

My eyes darted to my brother who clearly hadn't heard what Des was offering up—I hoped. "You're not serious."

Pulling back, she smiled wickedly, "Try me!"

"Kerrigan, party of four. Your lanes are ready." The announcer put a kibosh on Des' offer as I shrugged my shoulders.

"I can fuck you in the bathroom at home."

"I'll hold you to that, Odysseus." She kissed me again before standing and walking out of the bar with Lucy by her side.

"I thought I had the horny one. Shit, O. She may put you in an early grave. And you wanted an older woman?" Heath started cracking up as I shoved him away from me.

"Shut the fuck up. Forget you heard any of that!"

"Mum's the word, Odysseus." He exaggerated saying my name, putting a female tone on it. I couldn't help but laugh at him. "Don't break your back in the bathroom later tonight." He jumped away before I could hit him.

A couple hours passed and the girls were beyond tipsy, though they both denied it. It wasn't exactly how I'd planned to spend my birthday, but it was somehow perfect. My brother, his wife—whom was one of my best friends—and my wife all doing something 'normal' was just what I needed.

We had lanes at the end of the alley and I was sitting at a high-top against the wall with her standing between my legs. She was smiling like I hadn't seen her smile—maybe ever—and I think I fell a little harder for her. It was no secret that I loved her, but I don't think she'd ever comprehend how much.

A slow song with a sexy beat started overhead, *Good For You* by Selena Gomez, and she leaned in and whispered the words in my ear. Turning, she made sure to rub her ass against me and applied pressure.

Lowering my head, I kissed her neck, and then whispered in her ear, "If you're that desperate for me to show you my 'O' face, why don't we get out of here?"

Her hands snaked behind her and ran up and down my length through my jeans. "I don't want to get out of here." She faced me again and resumed stroking me, "Maybe I want you to show me your 'O' face now." I shifted her slightly to make sure her body blocked sight of her hands to any onlookers.

Her silky, warm fingers dipped under the waistband of my pants and my hungry cock awaited her. Running her fingers over the tip, I couldn't help but close my eyes for a moment. "Des. I'm going to pull you out back if you don't stop."

Her deep blue eyes pulled back and challenged mine. "I dare you."

I was speechless and if she thought I wasn't up for the challenge, she was in for a surprise. I pulled her hand out of my pants, pushed her away from me, and stood. Looking to Heath, I bellowed, "Meet you at the car in twenty." Lucy seemed confused, but Heath just nodded and distracted her.

Des let out a small squeal as I pulled her behind me, our hands clasped together. It was close to midnight and we barged out the back door as I scoped out the parking lot. Heath actually parked in a pretty inconspicuous spot so I headed that way. When I got to the back of his car, I pressed her up against the back passenger door and buried my face in her neck as she pulled my hips closer. My eyes raked over the parking lot and I didn't see anyone around. *Thank God!*

Moving, I picked her up and sat her on the trunk. "Hmm. I like this O."

"You have no idea what you do to me."

Grabbing me through my jeans, she huskily said, "I think I do."

My hands traveled under her mini skirt and pulled her thong off. Sticking them in my pocket, I lowered my head and went right to work. My tongue dove in as she cooed and gripped the long strands of hair on the top of my head. She was soaking wet and it wasn't long before she was dripping down my chin. I pushed her back flat on the car as I buried two fingers inside her. Time was against us.

"Des! Come baby!"

"I'm close, O." She panted, "Yes, right there. Shit!" She writhed against my face, back arched off the car as I kept licking at her until she pushed me off of her. She got up on her elbows as I pulled her skirt down and chastised me. "This was supposed to be about *you!*"

Grinning at her, I shrugged my shoulders and then was surprised when she jumped off the car and turned the tables on me. She unbuckled my pants and whipped my pants and boxers down to the ground in one swift movement.

"Des?"

"Shut up, O. Enjoy your birthday blow job."

I wasn't one to argue and once her mouth sucked me into her mouth, all bets were off. She fondled every part of me and took me balls deep into her mouth. Jesus, I wasn't going to last long. My hands gently pulled her face back and forth, her eyes enticing me on. She'd never been so voracious. The thought of being caught, being the envy of every man, pushed me over the edge.

"Des! If you don't stop..." She sucked harder as her other hand caressed my balls. "Shit!" I fucked her mouth, my seed spurting down her throat as she moaned around me. "Christ, Des."

Just as quickly, she pulled away and hurled into the bushes behind Heath's car. *What the hell?* That'd never happened before. Hell, I'd always been impressed with her lack of gag reflex. She'd clearly had too much to drink. Pulling my pants back on, I then held her hair and rubbed her back.

She was embarrassed, "I'm sorry. That's a first."

"He's a little big to handle that deeply, Des." She rolled her eyes at me and smacked my chest. "Babe, you've had a lot to drink. It's ok." I pulled her to her feet and watched her eyes get big. Turning to follow her line of sight, I saw Heath and Lucy at the front of the car.

Before I could even warn Heath to shut his mouth, he began clapping. Des, who rarely blushed, did just that. Lucy punched Heath in the gut and told him to knock it off before asking Des if she was ok. The girls climbed in the back seat and I caught Heath's stare over the top of the car. His eyes and smile said it all and I just shook my head at him.

"Little bro's got game! I'm proud."

"Shut the fuck up." I winked, "Might just be better game than you have!"

When we got back to the house, Des took a quick shower and I jumped in after her. Hopping out, I used the crutch I kept on hand and emerged into the bedroom. She was sitting on the bed and looked embarrassed.

"Des, it's ok." I sat down and pulled her to me. She put her head on my shoulder as I said, "I was hoping to dance with you tonight and I didn't get the chance."

"I'm sorry. I did get you something for your birthday, but I forgot it. I'm a jerk."

"You're not a jerk. You can give it to me when we get home. Honestly, I thought you forgot."

She tilted her chin and kissed me. "How could I possibly forget?"

I leaned over her and grabbed my phone off the nightstand, turning it on for the first time since arriving. Making sure my alerts were off, I selected the song I wanted and pulled her under the covers. "Come here. I just want to hold you."

"*Just* hold me?"

"Ok, maybe more." *Only You Only You* by Matthew Perryman Jones began playing. "Heath listened to it a lot when he and Lucy were first married. I can't help but think of you."

"Odysseus Philip Kerrigan! Did you steal a song from them and now you're trying to pawn it off on me?" Her tone was light and teasing.

"Bet your ass I did."

"They have quite the history don't they?"

"Yes. Since they were teens."

"It's so romantic."

"I don't know. I think our story is more romantic." I kissed her temple as she settled against me.

When the song was over, she handed me the phone and asked, "Play it again. We're stealing their song!"

~ ODYSSEUS ~

~ CHAPTER 18 ~

The next day, we chilled on the deck as Lucy and Des nursed their hangovers. Des seemed to be taking it hardest and wasn't eating much. She had joked that she was getting too old to go out drinking like that and the cougar jokes began to flow freely. It was all in good humor and she threw back the insults without hesitation.

That night we grilled some chicken and Des barely ate half of her serving. I was getting concerned that maybe she was sick. "Baby, you ok? Why don't you go lay down?"

"No, it's fine. I'll survive."

Heath and Lucy both looked at me like they knew some secret I didn't. Des was oblivious, just playing with her food. Curiosity got the better of me and I looked at them and asked, "What?"

Lucy didn't say anything and went back to eating, but Heath always had something to say. "So, when are you due Des?"

Due? What the hell was he talking about?

"Heath!"

He turned to Lucy and chided her, "You're thinking it, too."

Des just stared at them, growing pale.

"Mind your own business, Heath. They just got married, no need to pressure them about kids. You know how we felt about it, so back off." Heath went back to his food as I realized what they were implying.

Looking to my wife, my voice low, "Des?"

She rolled her eyes and laughed it off. "I'm not pregnant. Calm down."

The weight that dropped on me had suddenly been lifted. "Thank God! I'm way too young to be tied down with a kid." I hadn't even realized what I'd said until Lucy berated me after Des left the table.

"O, what is wrong with you? You know she already feels like she's too old for you, then to say what you just said..." For the first time ever I saw disappointment in Lucy's eyes when she looked at me. "Have you guys even talked about having kids? She *is* older and it's probably different for her."

I ran my hands through my hair as guilt racked me. I wanted Des whether that meant kids or not. I just hadn't thought about having them anytime soon. "I should go talk to her."

Lucy jumped up, volunteering, "Stay here. Let me check on her first. It might help having a woman to talk to." I was more than willing to let Lucy calm the waters with Des.

Heath and I sat there for a while in silence when I asked, "Have you and Lucy discussed kids?"

He eyed me carefully, like he was contemplating what to say. "I never wanted kids with anyone but her. But I also want to enjoy her and us. We haven't told anyone, so this stays here, but we're trying. Kind of."

"Kind of?"

"We're not preventing it anymore. We're looking at houses though mom and dad said we could stay here. The gym is up and running and it just seems like the next logical step."

"I had no idea. Though I don't think someone should have kids just because it seems like the next logical step." After over a year of marriage, maybe having kids *was* the next logical step for them. What did I know?

He grinned, "Would you rather be surprised and not expecting it at all? Because that's what almost happened here when you thought she might be pregnant. And you weren't exactly happy about that possibility, O."

Sighing, "Shit. I don't know. I mean, I think it'll happen when it's supposed to."

"If you're not using protection and you haven't discussed it, it's going to happen before you know it." I didn't say anything and I knew he was right. Des and I had a lot to talk about. He stood and began clearing the table. "Relax. It's going to be fine. Just give her some space."

Des was pretty quiet for the rest of the evening, but I knew she was upset and I had a feeling something else was bothering her. We had yet to talk and I knew we needed to. We were getting ready for bed when I wrapped my arms around her and gazed at our reflection in the bathroom mirror. She didn't react like she normally did and I knew I was in deep shit. Pushing away, she picked up her phone again. She'd been on it all weekend.

"Put it down, Des. We're on vacation." I'd turned my phone off the minute I walked into the house the day before. "Is something going on at work?" She was on edge, it was spilling off of her like a nasty odor.

"No. Everything's fine."

She was hiding something, but I wasn't going to push her. "You're lying. What is it?" I lied, I was going to push her.

"O, please."

"If this is about earlier and the kid thing, I'm sorry. I didn't mean it the way it sounded." I took a deep breath, willing her eyes to meet mine, but they wouldn't. "Are you pregnant?"

Her eyes finally snapped to mine. "How did it sound O? How did you mean it?" She was pissed. "I'm going to be thirty five in a couple weeks. Did you know that I'm considered advanced maternal age?" I had no idea what that meant and she knew it by the look on my face. "The risk and complications practically double with pregnancy once you're *my* age. But *you*, you can father kids until you're old and grey."

"Des, we need to talk about this. I want kids, I just didn't know if you did. We haven't talked about it. If you don't want them, fine. If you do, even better. But we *just* got married."

"I don't know if this is going to work out."

I closed the distance between us and grabbed her face. "Des, what's going on? Something's wrong. Please talk to me."

"I just, I can't do this." She pulled her face out of my hands and tried walking around me.

"Do what? I love you, Des. We can do this, but I need to know what you're talking about."

"You deserve more than me."

"How could I ask for more when you're everything to me? You!"

"You don't understand! I'm so fucked up in the head. I can't *do* love. Love abused me, took advantage of me, hurt me..." I tried to not look at her like she was crazy. The last thing I needed was her thinking I wanted to lock her up. But she refused to let me get a word in. "I'm standing here waiting for the other shoe to drop. Waiting for the moment you change your mind. I can't go through that kind of hurt again."

I reached for her, tears in my eyes, "Des. Love saved you, love cherishes you. He wasn't love. I am." I tried touching her, reassuring her, but she kept resisting me. "You're being irrational..."

She lurched back, "No. You can't fix this. You can't fix me. I'm entirely rational!" She was panting, on the verge of hyperventilating as tears seared both our cheeks. "I'm broken. You deserve someone who can love you right."

Was it possible to have a nervous breakdown in your mid-thirties, because that's what seemed to be happening with her? I was standing in front of a girl who I loved unconditionally, but she was doing everything she could to sabotage that love. She seemed momentarily disoriented and I seized the opportunity to grab hold of her. Then she said what I was afraid of, what I suspected was going through her head, and I don't even know if she knew she said it out loud.

"I have to leave you, before you leave me."

I couldn't hold her up and she took us both to the floor, but I never let go of her. Talking into her hair, I pleaded with her, "I'm not leaving you. Ever. Des, you're not broken and I wouldn't want to fix you even if you were. I love you. All of you. Every scar, bruise, demon, and thing you've done wrong; I love all of it. Without those things I wouldn't have you now. Why can't you accept that?"

"Because good things only happen to me for a short time. They never last."

"God dammit, Des. I'm not Saul!" I didn't mean to say his name, but I knew that he was what this whole argument was about. He'd fucked her up so bad that he'd destroyed her definition of love. And what scared me more was that I didn't know how to fix it.

She became quiet and relaxed in my arms. I wasn't sure if she'd conceded or if absolute exhaustion had claimed her. Managing to get us to our feet, I walked her to the bed. Removing her pants, I then covered her up and crawled in next to her. She was asleep within moments and so was I.

When I woke in the morning, she was still sleeping. I busied myself with cleaning the house, knowing the rest of the family would be arriving soon. Heath was at the gym and Lucy had the day off. If they had overheard our fight, Lucy didn't say anything. Knowing the garbage collection was coming in a few hours, I gathered all the waste baskets.

Quietly, I entered the room Des and I were occupying to grab the garbage and I found her packing her bag. "What are you doing?"

"O, please. I can't do this. It's too much pressure."

"What's too much pressure? What are you talking about?"

She waved her arms around the room, hollering, "This, all of this. Your whole family for the next two days. I'm just not ready."

"You're making excuses. My family loves you." I grabbed the waste basket from the bathroom, thinking she'd calm down and when I stepped back out she was marching out of the bedroom with her bag over her shoulder. "God dammit, Des!" I raced after her but didn't reach her until she was on the porch.

She threw her bag in the trunk of her car and slammed it shut. Turning to look at me, she just stared at me. Setting the basket down, I made my way to her. She put her hand up and said, "I just need a minute." She walked back past me and sat on the porch swing. I moved toward her and she demanded, "Alone."

I stroked her hair and reiterated everything I felt for her. "I love you. Nothing can change that. My family loves you. Whatever's bothering you, I can't help if I don't know. Take all the time you need. I'll be inside waiting." She just nodded.

I walked back inside and Lucy was in the kitchen cutting up some veggies. She made eye contact with me and half smiled, letting me know she knew we were fighting, but that she wasn't going to pry either.

"I don't know how to help her," I whispered.

"Maybe you're not the one who can." Her words took me aback. "I know it's not my business, but has she seen a therapist? I mean, I don't know if I could recover from everything she's been through and I imagine if I did, I'd need help."

"Honestly, I don't know."

"You saw one, right?"

"Yes. I know. It makes sense." I groaned, running my hands through my disheveled hair.

Lucy placed her hand on my forearm, sighing, "I don't know her very well, but I really like her. She's been through a lot. The mention of pregnancy really got to her last night. Did you talk at all?"

"I asked her if she was pregnant and if she wanted kids. But she just kept going on about how she wasn't worthy, or some shit, and that she had to leave me."

"Oh, O. I'm so sorry."

The sound of a car door slamming and then tires peeling out garnered the attention of us both. Had she overheard us talking? Leaping off the bar stool I'd been sitting on, I scrambled for the door. Her Challenger was at the end of the drive and then gone as I screamed her name.

"God dammit!" Still standing on the porch, I kicked the waste basket at my feet and another can, sending the contents flying. "Motherfucker!"

I turned my phone on and shoved it back in my pocket while it loaded then began to clean up the mess I'd made. "It's ok, O. I got it."

"No, I made the mess. I can clean it up."

We both picked up the scattered garbage and my eyes were drawn to a pink and white stick. That wasn't what I thought it was, was it? Picking it up, I looked at it closely. 'Pregnant' was displayed on the tiny screen. Lucy was pregnant? Lucy was pregnant! I began to wonder if Heath knew and then felt guilty that maybe I knew before he did. I watched Lucy pick up the last few items and put them in the large trash bin. My eyes drifted to her belly before she walked back inside.

I placed the test in my pocket and walked back inside. Lucy and I had a pretty candid friendship so I had to let her know that I knew. "Lucy?"

She turned back toward me, "What's up?" then made her way to the kitchen.

"Listen, I'm just going to lay this out in the open. Mum's the word." I pulled the pregnancy test out and laid it on the counter. "Does he know?"

She looked at me, confusion written all over her face. "What do you mean does *he* know?"

"Heath mentioned you guys were trying." She just stared at me, "Lucy, it says you're pregnant. Have you told Heath?"

She picked it up and looked at it, then back at me. She narrowed her eyes and with a smirk scoffed, "O, this isn't mine."

"What do you mean it's not yours?"

She pursed her lips at me and sighed. "O, think about it. I know you're not that dense." I just stared back at her dumbfounded. There was no way. "Des asked for a test yesterday, but I wasn't sure if she'd taken it yet or not. Congrats, O. Ready or not, you're going to be a daddy!"

I dropped my head to my hands and whispered, "Fuck. That's why…" I had asked her last night during her meltdown, but she never confirmed or denied it.

"She admitted to me after dinner last night that she suspected she might be. That's why she reacted so badly when you said there was plenty of time to discuss having kids. It dawned on her yesterday after being so sick all day. Clearly, it was more than a hangover. Anyway, I have some tests on hand and gave her one, though I didn't know she'd taken it."

"I have to fix this."

I rushed to the bedroom and grabbed my keys. Notifications galore started pinging on my phone. I checked my texts and none were from her. Then it began ringing and I answered without even looking at the number.

"Des?" It wasn't Des. It was the police station.

"Mr. Kerrigan?"

"Yes?"

"Have you spoken to your wife?" My stomach sank. Something was terribly wrong.

"No, no I haven't."

I heard the groan before he mentioned that he'd spoken to Des yesterday and that she'd assured him that I would call him right back. Somehow Saul had escaped. He'd been 'injured' and was transported to the hospital. He'd disappeared in the early morning hours yesterday. He could be anywhere. And she knew.

His trial was to start that next week, which was part of the reason I'd brought Des up to the lake house. We both needed the distraction and didn't need to be at the court house for a couple days.

Trying to keep my cool, I yelled in the phone, "She's out there alone. I need you to put an APB out for her. I'm going after her now. I'll be in touch." I hung up the call and barreled through the house.

"LUCY!"

"O, what's wrong?"

"He escaped and Des is out there alone."

"Oh my, God!"

"Stay in the house and lock the door. Don't you open it for ANYONE but Heath. Call him now and get him home."

She started throwing questions at me and all I did was react. I ran out the door, dialing Des as I went. I loved her, but her bravery—or stupidity—was starting to piss me the fuck off. Yet again, she was running from me in order to protect me, but putting herself in more danger and now our child, too. I had to find her before he did. I couldn't let myself think about her carrying my child *and* being out there unprotected. I had to focus on the task at hand.

Find Des.

Kill Saul.

Save my marriage.

Not necessarily in that order.

She was my heart and I couldn't survive without her.

SOUL

~ DESIREE ~

~ CHAPTER 19 ~

I sat on the porch swing trying to rationalize my thoughts. As long as O left his phone off, he wouldn't know that Saul had escaped. But if I left that would result in him turning his phone on. Closing my eyes, I took a deep breath. *I should just tell him.* But what to tell him, about the baby, Saul, or both? The baby was a pleasant surprise, but I'd been surprised before to just have it taken away again. My hand drifted to my belly as I reminded myself not to get attached to this pregnancy like I had the others.

Standing, I made my way to the open front door and overheard Lucy asking O if I'd seen a therapist. Anger, fear, and sadness filled me. Did I need therapy? Probably. But what good was therapy going to do as long as Saul was still out there? That was it. Decision made.

I hopped in my car and took off. He could turn his phone on, chase after me, but that didn't mean I'd answer or that he'd find me. I'd make sure he wouldn't; not until Saul was dead. There was no way I was going to let him hurt O or anyone in his family again. Over my dead body. It was time to be my own hero.

I didn't believe for one minute that Saul had fled far. He was close, probably closer than any of us thought. First thing I had to do was get some things from home, my gun included. If Will was still there, I'd have to wait until he left to go up north. Hopefully he would already be gone and I'd be gone before O found me there.

I knew that O would be livid with me, but I didn't see any other way around it. Saul wanted me and this was the only solution I could come up with. The question was where to start. Maybe he'd reach out to me before I really had to search for him. I was playing a risky game and I knew it. I needed somewhere to think and go over my plan.

Calling Stacey, I asked if I could crash at her place. It turned out she was at her parent's for the weekend, but called the super and gave him permission to let me in. Stacey had a set of keys inside and told me I was free to stay as long as I needed. She attempted to ask if everything was ok and I told her it was, that I just needed a couple days to sort through some things.

A couple days passed. I'd purchased a throwaway cell phone and was keeping my other one off. I knew O would be calling me and looking for me and this was the only way to keep him away. If I saw his calls flashing on the screen, eventually I'd cave. The only ones who knew my whereabouts were the police and they'd agreed to my plan. I would be the bait so that we could find Saul, only I had other things in mind for Saul.

They agreed to keep O out of it as much as possible. It was the only way I'd agree to everything. I had their protection and O had it, too. He just didn't know it. I kept my 'condition' to myself and lied through my teeth after the detective said O mentioned I was pregnant.

"It's not true. I thought I might be, but I'm not." The detective glared at me as I shook my head. "I wouldn't jeopardize a baby." Guilt racked me, but I had to push it aside. We'd never be safe, any of us, until Saul was dead.

I almost always had a tail and I had to take a leave of absence from work knowing that O, and possibly Saul, would both look for me there. I'd been put up in a safe house that didn't feel safe at all. It was a dump and I struggled to sleep—missing O and the way he kept me warm.

Detective Rollins stopped in to the crummy place on my third night there. Almost a week had passed since last I saw O. The detective had interesting information for me that night.

"We think that the cash buyer for your apartment is Saul. We're looking into it further."

Shaking my head, "It doesn't surprise me. He's demented like that." My brain started moving in warp speed as I mumbled, "That's why the buyer wanted the furnishings." A wave a nausea hit me as I stood and excused myself.

Rushing to the bathroom, I turned on the faucet and splashed cool water on my face. I couldn't even remember when I'd had my last period, but was pretty sure it was after the wedding—I think. I could be newly pregnant or close to the second trimester. A tiny balloon of hope filled me thinking I could be close to the end of my first trimester. If that was true, it'd be the longest any of my pregnancies had lasted.

There was a knock on the door. "Mrs. Kerrigan, are you alright?"

"Yes, I'll be right out." I'd never been this sick before either. Sighing, I had to stop thinking about it. The only thing I knew for certain was that this baby was O's.

I stepped out of the bathroom to find Detective Rollins on his cell. Walking to the kitchen, I grabbed a bottled water out of the fridge and sat down at the table. Soon after he disconnected the call and sat down across from me.

"It looks like Saul has someone helping him."

That was something I had been slightly suspicious of, but never gave much merit to. "Ok, so what now?"

"Do you have any thoughts?"

I rubbed my temples while I thought about it. "His parents are gone, left him a fortune," I flexed my neck from side to side. "My best guess is maybe one of his partners. He's a charmer and even after the PPO they never believed he was dangerous, probably still don't."

"Ok. We'll start there." He got up, leaving, and I collapsed on the couch and watched mindless TV.

I couldn't stop my mind from drifting to O and his family. If I managed to get out of this alive, would they ever forgive me? I didn't know, but it was a risk I had to take in order to keep them all safe. Then I wondered if O would even take me back. From his perspective I'd already betrayed him once for the sake of his own safety. I didn't know if he'd forgive me for doing it twice.

Tears drying on my cheeks, I gently rubbed my belly. The changes were only noticeable to me, but they were there. Usually a stomach sleeper, it was growing uncomfortable, like sleeping on a tennis ball. My breasts felt fuller and soon my nipples would become almost unbearable to touch. And that night out with Lucy, Heath, and O I'd had way too much to drink. I was an idiot. How could I have not noticed the signs earlier?

I pulled out my personal cell phone and turned it on against my better judgement. I had over thirty text messages and over a dozen voicemails. A majority of both were from O with a few from his mother, Lucy, Stacey, and my parents. Instead of listening to them, I dialed O's cell.

My heart was pounding in my chest so forcefully, it ached, as I waited to see if he would take the call.

"Des? Are you there?" Closing my eyes, his voice stirred emotions in me that I thought I'd be able to control. "Baby, please talk to me. Are you safe? I'm losing my mind."

"I'm safe. Please know how much I love you."

"Des, please come home. I don't know what's going through that mind of yours, but I'm begging you..."

"I can't. Not until he's gone. I love you, Odysseus. Please forgive me." As I hung up the phone, gut-wrenching sobs wracked my body. I immediately turned my cell back off as my chest and throat ached and a headache began thrumming in my skull.

It would be so easy to go home to him, but he'd never let me continue my plan with Detective Rollins. I woke a few hours later and carried myself to the bedroom. Turning music on, I put *Breathe Me* by Sia and drifted to sleep again as her piano-filled ballad calmed me.

~ ODYSSEUS ~

~ CHAPTER 20 ~

Flying down the freeway, I couldn't find her. Damn her and that sports car. Of course maybe she'd taken a different route home. I kept hammering her cell phone and eventually it just started going straight to voicemail.

When I made it to the apartment, I felt deep down like I'd just missed her. I could almost smell her perfume in the air. Some of the dresser drawers hung open and I knew then she planned for me not to find her. Sitting on the edge of the bed I tried to focus. Where would she go? Taking a chance, I called Stacey. She told me that she hadn't heard from Des, but that if she did, she'd let me know.

An hour later she called me back. "O, she needs some space. I told her I wouldn't tell you anything, and I won't. But she's safe."

"Stacey, you don't understand."

"O, I do, but I can't get involved. If something changes, I'll let you know." She disconnected the call as I cursed out loud.

A couple hours later I walked back into the apartment to find Will there. "Why aren't you up north?"

"Lucy and Heath filled me in when I got there. I couldn't stay up there knowing I could be of more help here."

Slamming the door shut, I grunted, "Thanks." Walking right to the fridge, I grabbed a beer and downed almost the entire thing in one long gulp.

"Is there any news?" I just shook my head. "O, I don't understand. What's going on, she's pregnant?"

It set me off. "Fucking Heath and Lucy! They can't keep their mouths shut about anything."

"They're just trying to help."

Pulling a second beer out, I offered one to Will and he passed. "Honestly, I don't know. I found a positive pregnancy test this morning and Lucy claims it's not hers. Des wouldn't confirm it, but I said something stupid when I thought she might be." Dropping myself to the couch, I lowered my head back and closed my eyes. "She knew that he escaped. She's up to something and I have to stop her. She's going to get herself killed."

"Have you talked to the police?"

Nodding, "Yes. That's where I just came from. They put out an APB for her, but they can't report her missing for twenty-four hours." He started to object, "Yes, even knowing Saul's out there. Believe me, I lost my shit."

"I'm sorry. I wish I knew how to help."

"Having you here helps. I appreciate it, man."

We watched ESPN for a couple of hours before I decided to crash. I tossed and turned that night clutching her pillow. I finally gave up on sleep as the sun rose and headed down to the gym. One of the perks of being an employee, and it being a holiday, was that the gym was empty. It was too early for most of the regulars anyway.

The next few days came and went with the same course of events. I'd call her, leave voicemail, text her, call and drive by her work, as well as visit the police station. All I got in return was nada. I was beginning to think the cops were in on it all. The cops had to know something, right? She couldn't have just vanished into thin air. Her work told me that she'd taken a leave of absence, but that was all they could tell me. With each day that passed I grew more and more scared for her and what Saul would do to her if he found her. But I couldn't let my mind wander down that path.

That Friday I was sitting at home, already six beers into the case I bought. Drinking heavily wasn't my typical course of action, but my fear for her was turning into anger that was starting to boil over. Will walked in that night with Dorian, D, and Heath with him. They all just nodded at me and began the ritual of setting up to play poker. It'd been a long time since all five of us had played together.

D and Dorian set up the poker table, Will ordered pizza and Heath loaded the fridge with more beer. They were all sitting around the table waiting for me. Glaring at them, I pulled myself up and plopped down in the empty chair. Everyone had their cash on the table, turned it in for chips and I did the same. Dorian then dealt and the game began.

I was drunk, or at least getting there. We'd ordered three large pizzas and they were gone along, with my case of beer, and we'd put a pretty big dent into a second case. Pretty sure I was down sixty bucks and I was hurting for chips. I just wasn't in the right mindset and gave no fucks about winning. My phone started ringing and I pulled it out of my pocket, curious to who'd be calling.

When I saw her name flash across the screen, adrenaline pumped through me, sobriety trying to take hold of me. I dropped the phone on the table trying to get it to answer, which got the attention of my brothers. Frantically, I put it to my ear.

"Des? Are you there?" She wasn't speaking and I was worried this was some horrible joke. "Baby, please talk to me. Are you safe? I'm losing my mind."

"I'm safe. Please know how much I love you."

If you love me, why'd you leave? But I couldn't ask her that, not now. "Des, please come home. I don't know what's going through that mind of yours, but I'm begging you..."

"I can't. Not until he's gone. I love you, Odysseus. Please forgive me."

"Des? Des!" I checked the screen to see the call had ended. Chucking it across the room, I roared, "GOD DAMMIT!" and watched my only source of communication with her shatter on the floor. "FUCK!"

My brothers just sat and waited. We'd all been pissed off beyond reproach before and we all knew that I just needed a few minutes to cool down. They began talking quietly amongst themselves as I staggered to the fridge. I needed something more potent and found her bottle of fireball in the freezer. Yanking it out, I removed the lid and chugged.

Sitting back down at the table I began rambling, "I love you O, please forgive me O...what the fuck is wrong with that woman?"

Will asked, "Did she say anything else?"

I sat and recounted our brief exchange. "She said something about not coming home until he was gone. Dammit. The cops have to be in on this. I just know it. They're fucking using her as bait and she's letting them."

"That's just not right. Not with her..." I glared at Heath and he shut up.

Dorian, always way too intuitive, "Not with her what?"

"Not with her history with him. She's too fragile." Heath recovered quickly and Dorian seemed to buy it.

"Listen. I have a client who's a PI. I can call him and see if he can find anything out." I looked at Dorian, not sure what to say. "O, it's no problem. He has some connections at the station and may be able to help us out. At least give you some peace of mind if the cops are using her as bait or not."

I just nodded my head and took another swig of the cinnamon whiskey before passing it around the table. They all took their turns with the bottle, D having the worst reaction.

"What the fuck? That shit is nasty." We all chuckled.

Turning the music up, my thoughts wandered as *Angel* by Theory Of A Deadman played. The bottle hung in my hands as the words cut me like a knife. I was a soldier, trained to serve and protect, but she didn't want me to do that for her. It's as if she was determined to save herself. I admired that in her, but sometimes we all needed someone, no matter the possible consequences we might face.

Des was part of me, always would be, but maybe she had one thing right. I couldn't save her. She had to save herself. And that involved more than physical danger. It involved her spirit, her soul, and her mind. Nobody could free those if she didn't want them to be free. She was her own prisoner in a cell of her own making and nobody would be able to help her escape except herself.

I took another swig to find the bottle empty. *Fuck.* I set it on the table as my vision blurred. Then I tried speaking and found I couldn't form words like I should've been able to. Soon I was aware of two bodies flanking me and dragging me out to the balcony. The cool night air assaulted me and I hurled over the deck. I was known for holding my liquor, but every man had his limits.

Shortly after, I was being placed in bed as Heath—or maybe it was Will—told me to get some rest. I was way too drunk to give a shit which one it was, and to be honest, I couldn't tell in this condition.

I woke in the morning to Heath next to me and shoved his ass out of the bed. He hit the floor with a thud and jumped to his feet, fists in the air.

"What the fuck?" His eyes focused on mine as I laughed.

"I don't need you keeping me warm, fucker."

Shaking his head, "I wasn't keeping you warm, asshole. I was making sure you didn't drink yourself into a fucking coma." He walked to the bathroom and reminded me, "Besides, it's my fucking bed, not yours."

"Yeah, yeah." The pounding in my head took over as I closed my eyes.

"Here." Opening one eye, I saw Heath holding out a glass of water and a bottle of pills. "Take it. Might help. Though you deserve every minute of that hangover." He walked out of the room and left me to my misery.

I took a deep breath and prepared myself for the fight of a lifetime. I wasn't going to give up on her. Dorian said he had a client who could help. After I showered, I headed to the kitchen to find Dorian still there. Apparently everyone stayed over and I wasn't the only one nursing a hangover.

Dorian had his sunglasses on and was drinking a cup of coffee. Joining him, we talked about his client. He called him and set up an appointment for later that day. Hitching a ride with him, our first stop was the cell phone store. I needed a new phone immediately.

Operation 'Find Des' was underway, again.

~ DESIREE ~

~ CHAPTER 21 ~

The next day I couldn't get what Detective Rollins had said out of my head. They suspected that Saul was the one who bought my place. That had to be where he was hiding, maybe. Was he that stupid or did he just not anticipate them finding that out? There was no way the cops would let me walk in there without backup and I knew there was no way Saul would confront me if I had backup. I had to try to get away on my own, but how?

My security detail made it exceptionally easier for me than I anticipated. I found him asleep on the couch and went back to my room. Arranging the pillows under the covers, I walked right out the front door without waking him. I'm sure it helped that he had the TV on as loud as he did.

I had ample protection, at least that's what I told myself, my gun and knife both in my purse. When I pulled up to my old building a chill ran over me, like I could sense he was close. I tucked the knife in my boot and left the gun in my purse. Taking a deep breath, I walked into the building under the darkness of night.

I still had my key and it didn't appear like the locks had been changed, so I tried the key. It worked. Walking in, nothing had changed. It was like I'd never left, like a shrine. *Oh, God. What if I was wrong and I was walking into my old place and found a little old lady living here?* This was a mistake. I had to go. As I turned back toward the door, he was there.

Immediately, I backed away and reached for my gun, but he already had one pointed at me. "You're brave. Stupid, but brave." He sneered at me as my stomach revolted.

"I could say the same about you."

Waving the gun toward the couch, he ordered, "Sit down."

"You sit down." He didn't want me dead, not yet anyway.

"Where's the gun? Your purse or behind your back?"

"I don't have a gun, Saul. You know I hate them."

Walking closer he circled around to my side as his eyes traveled my body. "Something's different. What is it?"

"Nothing's different. You can't be here. The cops suspect that you bought the place, they'll be here soon."

Shrugging his shoulders, "Perfect, that means I can use you as my shield. I mean, you're the reason I'm in this mess to begin with." Trailing his finger down my cheek he whispered, "So many lies, Des. And for what? Because you feel sympathy for that cripple?"

"Don't you call him that! He's more of a man than you could ever hope to be." I expected the smack that came, but not the yanking on my hair that followed.

"You're going to pay for what you've done."

"Not if you pay first."

Before I could really fight back, everything went black.

I woke on the living room floor, to his hands attempting to move me. There was no way he was going to lay another hand on me without me fighting back. The struggle began again as I reached into my purse. He was still trying to get control of me when I pulled it out, but he spotted it too soon. We began to grapple and he managed to knock the gun from my hand as we hit the floor.

I tried to scurry after it, not entirely sure where it'd gone, when I felt his body on top of mine. Kicking out at him, I made contact with his chest and crawled away from him.

"You stupid bitch. You're going to pay and so is your cripple."

I spotted my gun just before he started dragging me toward the bedroom. Glancing up, his eyes were focused on the bedroom and I didn't see his own gun, so I reached for the knife in my boot, my scalp on fire from where he gripped my hair. Flipping the switchblade open, I lunged toward him and pierced the back of his thigh before pulling it out and slashing at his hand.

Saul screamed out and released me as he reached for the wound now spurting blood from his leg. With him momentarily distracted, I scrambled for my gun and almost had it when searing pain ripped through my left leg. I had to keep moving forward. Finally my fingers circled the gun just as he flipped me over. Sitting astride me, his hands reached for my neck as I kept my hand out of his line of sight.

"I'm going to enjoy the look on his face when he realizes you're dead."

Gasping, I choked out, "Not if I don't enjoy the look on his face when he finds out you're dead first!"

I wasn't leaving this apartment until he was dead, knowing I might be dead along with him. Pulling my hand out from under the chair, I aimed and pulled the trigger. He leapt back and I had no idea where I'd hit him or how badly. With the gun still in my hand, he reached into his pocket as he backed up toward the bedroom. The second I saw the silver barrel emerging from his pocket, I fired again. This time I saw the blood pour out of his chest.

He looked down at the wound and continued to stumble backward and into the bedroom. Pulling his gun out, he aimed, but not at me. I followed his line of sight and saw a red gallon jug sitting by the front door. It was gasoline and it wasn't till then that the smell infiltrated my nostrils.

"Bye bye, Des."

"Saul, NO!"

We both fired at the same time. Me at him and him at the explosive. I was thrown against the wall from the force of the blast, and watched him stumble back out of sight. Making my way toward the bedroom, limping, and away from the flames now consuming the living room, I found him sitting on the edge of the bed. Blood dripped from his mouth and his shirt was saturated with it. The gun was in his hand and I aimed mine at him once more.

"Drop it, Saul."

"You'll always be *my* Buttercup..." An attempt at a chuckle escaped his lips as he saw me cringe.

He lifted his arm and I shot him again, this time in the head. Point blank range. His body fell onto the bed and I just stood there, shock taking hold of me. Moving to lean against the bedroom wall, the pain in my leg reverberated through me. I had to focus.

I could see the morning rays peering through the windows. After he knocked me out I must've been out for a while. Looking back toward the living room, there was no way out; I was doomed. The flames already spreading. But, Saul was dead. Finally, I'd done what no one else could. I'd wiped his despicable soul from existence.

I stood there watching as the flames crept up the walls just outside the bedroom, his motionless body would soon be nothing but ashes and mine along with his. Closing the bedroom door, I hoped it'd give me some time, though I wasn't sure what time I needed. Sliding down, I sat on the floor, resolved to the fact that I was going to die along with the baby in my belly. O would never know, but at least he would be safe. Body, heart, and soul; my willing sacrifice for him. He was young and he'd find love again.

I sat there listening to the fire take control of my surroundings. The sobs tore through me and then the smoke started getting to me. My lungs burned as I held my shirt over my mouth trying to catch my breath. I wanted to call O, but my purse was in the living room, along with my phone.

"DES!"

Now I was losing it, the lack of oxygen warping my senses. I heard the snapping and crashing of wood hitting the floor outside the bedroom.

"DES!"

O? Panicked, I crawled closer to the bedroom door. "O?"

"Des! We have to get you out."

"What are you doing here? Get out, O!" The door flew off the hinges and there he was, my knight in shining armor, my soldier, smoke billowing around him. The only thing separating us were more flames. The fire had already spread and the doorway was engulfed. "O, get out of here."

"I'm not leaving you." He glanced at the bed and back to me. "You have to jump!"

I was still on the floor, shaking my head. I had to get him out of here. "I can't." I was pretty sure my leg was broken. Before I could gather the strength to try, he backed up and jumped into the room. "O!"

He pulled me to my feet and realized I was favoring my left leg. "You're hurt."

"Leave me O. You have to get out."

"I'm not leaving you," his hand came down to rest on my belly, "either of you. We're in this together, till the end."

He knew? "You know?"

"Lucy told me. Des, we have to get out of here. Do you trust me?"

I was sobbing and clinging to him, "Of course I trust you."

He ran into the bathroom and emerged a few moments later with wet towels. "Wrap this around your mouth. We have to go out the way we came." He helped me tie the towel and then asked, "Can you walk?"

"I'll try."

"We're getting out of here, baby." He kissed me chastely and then he jumped back through the frame where the door no longer hung. Reaching his hand to me, "Come on, Des. I got you."

Snubbing the pain, I jumped through the door and took in what used to be my apartment; unrecognizable from the smoke and flames that were consuming it. A horrible creak sounded from above us. His body covered mine as I looked up and saw the beam split in two, falling on top of us. As I moved out from under his body, I realized he was unconscious with the beam pinning him to the floor.

"O!" No, no, no...this is what I was trying to avoid.

"Is there anyone in here?"

"Over here!"

Within seconds, a fireman was pulling me from the room as I screamed for O. "You have to get him out! He's my husband!" A second fireman appeared and I was handed over to him like a ragdoll while the other one went back in for O.

I tried fighting the paramedics, refusing treatment until they forced an oxygen mask over my face. "You have to take this. Don't make us restrain you."

Didn't they understand? My husband was still inside, the father of my unborn child, and there was no sign of him or the fireman. Windows shattered and flames burst into the sky. Then I saw him; the fireman emerged from the flames and had a body over his shoulder. I wasn't even sure if it was the same fireman, but I recognized the body. It was Saul.

Where was O? My heart stopped beating, my lungs stopped working as I stared at the empty space where O should've been standing. One of the firemen pulled his mask off and shook his head at another man in uniform. That was when I saw Dorian and Detective Rollins. How long had they been here?

Prying the mask off my face, I ran toward the firemen as the pain in my leg radiated through me. "Where is he?" He caught me as my leg gave way. "Go back!" They carried me back to the sitting ambulance and set me on the stretcher as I screamed for Dorian. "Dorian!" His eyes found me and he rushed over to me. "O's still in there." He didn't say a word, just vanished inside.

The pain was becoming too much. Oxygen was placed over my face again and everything started to spin. I couldn't lose him. This wasn't my plan. I was trying to protect him. My eyes closed and all I saw were his sad eyes smiling at me, only the way they could; flashing from green to gold. Now Dorian was risking his life for O's because he risked his life for me. I'd never forgive myself. I just wanted to die. They were all better off having never met me.

~ ODYSSEUS ~

~ CHAPTER 22 ~

Dorian and I were sitting across the desk from his client, the PI. His name was Judd according to the nameplate. He was on the phone with one of his contacts at the police station. I kept checking my phone and sending Des messages, hoping she'd respond. It was already late afternoon and the adrenaline pumping through me had my right leg bouncing up and down.

"Thank you, darling. I look forward to hearing back from you." He paused, "I think I can arrange that." He winked at Dorian and me as I shook my head. I knew it was part of the game, but if he was setting up a booty call, I didn't have time for it. "Talk to you soon."

He hung up the phone and I asked, "So?"

"She's looking into it. She said there's definitely something going on. She'll call me back."

"When?"

He shook his head, "It could be an hour or four. I suggest you go home, or whatever, and I'll call you as soon as I know something." I slammed my hands down on the desk. "Hey. I get it man, but my hands are tied. Beth is good and discreet. If there's info to be had, she'll get it."

Dorian chimed in, "Come on O. You heard the man." Resigning, I nodded as he turned back to Judd, "I really appreciate it. Thank you."

"You owe me Kerrigan!" He laughed and they shook hands before we headed out.

That night we did get an update. Des was working with the cops and was apparently in a safe house, but Beth didn't know where. She was still working on it. I bolted out of bed a few hours later when my cell rang. It was four in the morning. Answering the call, it was Judd.

"I have the address. I'll pick you up in twenty."

I didn't even respond, just started getting dressed and headed downstairs. Dorian was asleep on the couch and I didn't want to wake him. Seemingly I was too loud because he appeared at my side a few minutes later.

"You don't think you're going alone are you?"

"Judd says they have an address. I just didn't want to wake you."

He gripped my shoulder and gave it a reassuring squeeze. "Let's get your girl." Judd pulled up and we hopped into his sedan.

Judd warned us as we pulled up. "They're not going to take kindly to us showing up like this. Be prepared."

I banged on the front door and almost straightaway a man answered the door. He looked like he'd just woken up. "I want to see my wife!"

Lifting his chin, he snarled, "I don't know what you're talking about."

Judd stepped forward and called the officer by his name, though he wore no badge. "Timmy, is the girl here or not?"

"Shit. Dammit Judd." He opened the door grumbling, "I'm going to lose my fucking job because of you."

"Maybe so, but looks to me like you were sleeping on the job." We took in the dismal surroundings and the blanket on the couch signifying he'd been asleep there. "If you lose your job it won't be because of me."

Groaning, "This way. She's back here."

He pointed to a back bedroom and I made my way inside. She was asleep under the covers and I sat down next to her. "Des?" I placed my hand on her shoulder and quickly realized it was a coup. Yanking back the covers, I exposed a body of pillows. "What the fuck! Where is she?"

We turned on the lights and checked every nook and cranny for her. She was gone. Timmy discovered her car was also gone from out back. Anger got the best of me as I slammed him up against the wall. Dorian and Judd had to separate us as I screamed at him.

"Where's my wife, you prick?"

Dorian dragged me outside to catch my breath. "O, you have to relax. She's smart and underhanded. She probably marched her ass out with him asleep on the couch."

"That's what I'm worried about. She's too fucking daring for her own good." I couldn't help it as the sobs tore from me. "Dorian, she's pregnant."

He leaned back from me as my words sank in. Running his hand over his face and gripping his jaw, he whispered, "Jesus, O." Then he clasped me to his chest. "We'll find her."

Heading back inside, Timmy divulged more info. "They suspect that he bought her old place, but haven't had a chance to check it out."

"That's where she went. I know it." All three of them just looked at me. "He's attacked her there before. She knows he'll find her there. She's not stupid, unlike your department of incompetent dimwits. She's going to try to end this once and for all."

Judd agreed and we high-tailed it out of there, toward Des' old place. The sun was rising and shone bright hues of pinks and blues. Relief filled me when I spotted her car, but it was immediately replaced with dread. Smoke was billowing out of her end of the building. A few neighbors started running out the front door as I jumped out of Judd's sedan.

Running toward the front door, Dorian's hand came down on my shoulder. "O, you can't go in there."

Turning to him, "I can't leave her. If it was your wife, your unborn child, you'd do the same thing. I know you would." Dorian had lost a lot and there was no need to get into it further. He released me and I told him to call the cops. "Whatever happens, she's got to be the number one priority."

Pulling out his cell, he agreed and dialed 9-1-1. Opening the door, another neighbor ran out with her small dog wrapped in her arms. The smoke hit me like a wall. My eyes instantly burned and my lungs started coughing in protest. Finding the stairs, I began the trek up to her floor. *God damn this bum leg.* It took me longer than it should have, but there was nothing I could do about it.

Finally, I reached her floor and headed toward her end of the hall. Flames covered the ceiling as I crouched in front of her door. The knob was hot so I had no choice but to kick the door in. It gave quicker than I expected, but that was probably due to the damage the flames had done. Sprinklers were spraying from overhead, but they were no match for the inferno that blazed.

"Des!" Taking a deep breath, my arms around my head, I ran through the doorway. "DES!"

The bedroom door was closed and I was terrified about what I might find behind it. Memories from the desert flashed through my brain as I fought to push them away. Would I find the room empty, Des gone, or would she be dead as Saul waited for me? Hell, maybe he was dead, too. Fuck. I didn't know which scenario would be worse.

"O?"

Praise Jesus, she was alive...for now.

~ DESIREE ~

~ CHAPTER 23 ~

When I woke, my whole body ached and was stiff. Memories inundated me and I tried to push them away. The familiar sounds of a hospital floated around me, making it unnecessary to open my eyes to reveal where I was. O was gone and I didn't want to live this life without him. *The baby.* My hand drifted to my still flat abdomen. I didn't even know if the baby was still there. The only proof I'd had was a positive home pregnancy test. I wasn't sure how far along I was or how long I'd been in the hospital.

Not able to keep my eyes closed any longer, squinting as my eyes adjusted to the bright light, I found the clock. According to the date a couple days had passed. I spotted some flower arrangements on the window sill as a nurse walked in.

"Good, you're awake." She took my wrist in hers, asking, "How do you feel?"

Shrugging my shoulders, I retorted, "How should I feel?" She eyed me suspiciously before writing in my chart.

"I'll let your doctor and family know you're awake." She removed the catheter and I was grateful for the lack of discomfort. "If you have to go to the bathroom, ask for help. Ok?" I just nodded.

Then I remembered her mention my family. "Family?" I glanced to my left hand and my rings were nowhere to be found. "My rings?"

"Your family has those, too." She left before I could inquire anymore.

When I tried to move my legs, I felt the weight of the cast. *Shit!* I wasn't going to be able to go anywhere, not easily. The *family* was probably O's family and I didn't think I could bear to see them. I'd gotten their son killed, maybe two sons killed, and Will had almost been killed before. They should've abandoned me and had every right to do so.

I pulled myself to a sitting position and soon regretted it.

"My dear, where do you think you're going?" I looked up to see O's mom.

Tears threatened as O's eyes stared back at me. I'd never noticed before that he had his mother's eyes, though hers were more green than gold. I couldn't look at her and not cry. My hands covered my face and I soon felt her hand on my shoulder.

"Everything's ok, Desiree."

Sobbing, "How can you say that? I've lost him."

"Lost him? Lost who?" Was she being dense on purpose?

"O! I can't do this without him." Words started falling from my lips before I could stop them. "I'm not built to be a single mom. I can't do this alone."

"Shh, you're not alone. I know you and O have some things to work out, but he'd never abandon his child." My head ached. What was she talking about?

"Mom, can I have a minute?"

I needed to be committed. His voice filled the small room and when I lifted my head, he stood in front of me. His mom hugged him and then left the room. He was an apparition, a mirage, because my O was gone, dead, and it was my fault.

With the slightest limp, he came closer and sat on the bed next to me. Closing my eyes, I shook my head in denial.

"Des, please look at me."

"I can't look at you. You're not real."

His soft chuckle filled my ears like the sweetest song. "I am real and so are you."

Warm hands cupped my cheeks and stroked my face, only the way he could, as I leaned into his touch. Minty breath drifted over my face and his scent filled my nostrils.

"You're alive?"

"Nothing was going to take me from you."

Whimpering, his kiss silenced my cries. My hands reached for him in a frenzy as he leaned over me. "I thought you were dead." I buried my face in his neck as his hands dug into my back.

"I thought you were, too. Why'd you do it?"

I knew what he was referring to and just shook my head. "It was never going to end, not unless *I* ended it."

He pulled my face away until our eyes met. "Des, you're not alone." His eyes were filled with tears as he closed them and kissed the bridge of my nose. "I thought I lost you. When I saw the smoke, I..."

"I'm sorry. I couldn't risk you getting hurt."

"Why can't you understand that I feel the same way?" His voice filled with annoyance as he spit out, "For God's sake, Des. You walked in there knowing he was there and knowing you were pregnant with *my* child."

"Yes. I did. A child you said you didn't want!"

"Dammit!" He stepped away from me and ran his hands through his hair. "That's not what I meant. I just thought we'd have more time. You think I don't want to have children with you?"

I shook my head because I wasn't really sure. Maybe I'd taken his statement of wanting to wait as a threat that he didn't want kids at all. "I just thought... I'm sorry." My voice cracked again as more tears fell.

"I want you to be the mother of my children more than anything else in this world. Well, maybe not more than I want you. I can't breathe without you, Des. I try to think about a time when you weren't there and I can't. Life didn't exist for me until you. A child will just add to that."

Guilt like I'd never felt flowed through me. "I'm so sorry." So many problems could've been avoided had we taken the time to communicate with one another, trust each other wholly. Something not surprising since we were still getting to know one another.

He sat down next to me and pulled me to his chest. "I love you, Des. So fucking much. I'd walk through fire over and over again to prove it."

Looking up into his eyes I chastised him, "Walking through fire for me once is quite enough." I spotted the bandage on his arm and fingered it gently. "Is it bad?"

"I'll survive. As long as I have you."

"You always had me. I just wasn't sure you wanted me."

Sighing, "What do I have to do, Des to prove it to you? Do I need to jump on couches or take out a billboard?" He kissed my temple and whispered, "Stop trying to get rid of me."

"You're not getting rid of me." I cupped his face and kissed his lips. "I love you, O."

"I love you, too, baby." He laid down with me and soon I was drifting off again. "It's ok, Des. You need to sleep." And I did just that.

Later that day, after yet another nap, I was put in a wheelchair and taken to the O.B. floor, O by my side. The doctor had confirmed that my bloodwork was indeed positive for pregnancy.

"Based on your HCG levels, it looks like you're already in your second trimester, or close to it." If that was true, I had been pregnant for far longer than I realized. *"We'll take you to O.B. later today for an ultrasound."*

We officially spilled the news to his parents, Will, Heath, and Lucy. They were all very happy though I was pretty sure I recognized a slight sadness in Lucy's eyes. She'd told me that they'd stopped trying to prevent pregnancy, but weren't really 'trying' either. I think I understood how she felt. Had you asked me six months prior if I was going to have kids I would've been convinced it was never going to happen for me.

Now here I was, still a newlywed, and now pregnant.

With O's help, I lay back on the bed in the ultrasound room. The doctor came in and I recognized her as one of Saul's former coworkers. She just nodded and I could see the apology in her eyes, like she finally knew and understood everything he'd put me through. She was one of few who'd never been romantically involved with Saul, unlike her counterparts.

"Let's start with the Doppler and check for the heartbeat. With your bloodwork indicating you're close to the second trimester we should be able to pick up the heartbeat."

Cold jelly was squirted on my abdomen as she began to move the small wand over my belly. I was growing increasingly nervous as she continued to move it without finding the heartbeat. After several minutes, O took my hand as she put the Doppler away and pulled over the ultrasound machine.

"We're going to take a look, ok? Just as a precaution."

She didn't need to explain the concerns to me. I had the medical training and I was already preparing myself for the worst. I'd been through it too many times before. I watched the monitor above my head as she probed at my belly. I knew what I was seeing, but couldn't believe it. Was this really happening?

~ ODYSSEUS ~

~ CHAPTER 24 ~

I held her hand, petrified, though I couldn't show it. We'd almost lost each other because we'd both been so determined to protect the other, neither of us willing to budge. Now she was pregnant. I admit it was sooner than I wanted, but the thought of her belly swollen with the product of our love was almost overwhelming. I never thought I'd find anyone who'd accept me, let alone who'd want to bear my children.

The doctor broke into my thoughts as I wiped the sweat from my brow. "Well, now I see what's going on." Going on? What did she mean? She smiled at me and then at Des. "Right here, there's your baby." She zoomed in and a small dot on the screen was fluttering back and forth. "There's the heartbeat."

Des released a gasp that was a mix of relief and jubilation. I leaned down and kissed her forehead. "We're having a baby, Des!" It was like I hadn't fully believed it until that moment.

"Not just one baby." My eyes darted to the doctor, to the screen, to Des, and back. "Here's your other baby and the heartbeat. Looks like they're fraternal, but we won't know for sure without further tests. Congratulations!"

What the hell did she just say? Twins? Closing my eyes, I shook my head in disbelief.

"O? Are you ok?" I looked to Des, who had tears in her eyes. "Maybe you should sit down."

The nurse pushed the chair over behind me and I dropped down to it. "Twins? You're sure?"

The doctor smiled, "Yup. Looks like it's still pretty early. You're measuring about six to seven weeks along. The heartbeat can be hard to hear before eight weeks."

I was still trying to process everything, "But you said she was close to the second trimester because of her bloodwork."

"Yes." She looked to Des and smiled. "Desiree's bloodwork was elevated which typically indicates one of two things; how far along she is or a multiple pregnancy. We never assume multiples until we have the proof." Handing Des a printout with two circles, she confirmed, "There's your proof. I'll call for the orderly to get you back to your room. This is still a very delicate time in the pregnancy. Everything looks great, but you may want to keep the news that it's twins to yourself until you're closer to the second trimester."

"Got it. Thank you." The doctor and nurse left the room and Des sat up some and turned to me. "Are you ok?"

"Me? Yeah, I'm just...twins. Wow."

"O, if this is too much tell me now. I know you didn't sign up for this, not yet, and now we're having twins."

I jumped upright and sat down next to her. "Whoa, whoa, whoa. I just thought we'd have more time. This," I fingered the ultrasound pic, "this is amazing, baby. Epic." She smiled as tears filled her eyes. "I'm so overcome with love for you. You have no idea." I kissed her and kept our foreheads together, "Are *you* ok with this?"

She started sobbing and covered her face. Between broken breaths she confessed, "I want this more than you know. I gave up hope that it would happen, O. I'm so happy, but I'm terrified, too."

"Terrified? Why?"

I tilted her face so I could fully see her. She was avoiding my eyes as she revealed another secret. "I've had three miscarriages, all with Saul." She must've felt me tense, because she defended him, "It's not what you think. It was nothing anyone did, the pregnancies just didn't take. I've never made it into the second trimester. Now, it's twins. I'm scared to death, O. I don't know if I can go through this again."

Pulling her to me, I consoled her, "I'm so sorry. No matter what happens, Des, I'm here for you."

"Thank you. I'm here for you, too." She wiped at her tears and echoed my thoughts. "Twins!"

I wiped her tears as I said, "I probably should've told you twins run in the family."

Giggling, she retorted, "You should've reminded yourself when you decided to skip a condom. But, if they're fraternal that means I released two eggs, maybe more, and it had nothing to do with your DNA."

"More?"

"Calm down. Pretty sure there's just two in there." Her hand covered her belly and I in turn covered her hand.

"I hope so. Twins is one thing, but triplets. Good God!"

She looked reflective and whispered, "I think we should tell them it's twins, but I'm worried about Lucy."

"Worried about Lucy? Why?"

"Lucy confided in me that they've been trying with no luck. I feel like I'm rubbing it in her face."

"They've been trying? Heath just said they weren't preventing it. I had no idea. I'm sure she'll be supportive. It's not in her nature to be jealous."

"It's not about her nature, O. Heath is just going with the flow, but Lucy...Lucy wants a baby. It's a really hard thing for a woman. We're built to have babies and when it doesn't happen...it's just really hard."

I thought about what she said and began to understand. "I get it, I think. The doctor suggested we should wait to tell."

"I know, but I'm done with the secrets. I kept my previous pregnancies a secret from friends and family and I don't want to do that this time. I'd rather have their support and well wishes. If that makes sense."

"Perfectly. How do you want to tell them?"

"Let me think about it. I'm sure it'll come to me. Right now I just want to go home."

"Babe, I'm not sure they're discharging you today."

"Can't you break me out of here?" I looked at her casted leg, and then pulled up my pants exposing my prosthetic and raised my brows at her. Laughing, "We're quite the pair."

After more x-rays, the orthopedic gave Des a walking cast, but ordered her to take it easy and asked her to make an appointment for a couple weeks out to check the progress of her break. They discharged her late the next day. It was a process getting her up the stairs, but with Will's help we managed just fine.

"Where do you want to go babe, bedroom or couch?"

"Bedroom. I think I could sleep for days." Propping her up in bed, she removed the bulky walking cast leaving the bandage wrap on and slid under the covers. "Oh, my God. I never thought I'd be so happy to be back in this bed."

"Hmm." She eyed me and grinned. "Don't get any ideas. You need sleep."

Pouting, she asked, "Will you stay with me?" Her eyes were already growing heavy as I climbed in next to her. "Love you, O." She yawned and closed her eyes.

Stroking her hair and her face gently, I sighed in relief. She was home, she was safe, and Saul was dead. Life could finally move forward. And she was pregnant, with twins. *Holy shit!* It was still surreal. We hadn't told anyone we were expecting twins, but we had a plan to. Our life together was finally beginning, the way it should've from the start. But if that was the case, why was I so nervous something was going to wreck it? Maybe I'd just grown accustom to it, but I prayed with everything I had that our days of fear and hesitation were over.

Des slept the night away while I got a few hours of shut-eye. Horrible foreboding wouldn't let me be and I decided to take it out on my body at the gym. When I came back upstairs she was still sound asleep. I made my way to the bathroom and undressed. I turned the shower on, removed my prosthetic, and leaned against the shower wall.

I let the water beat down on me once I sat on the shower bench, my hair falling into my eyes as the water dripped off the ends. I didn't hear her enter the bathroom until the glass door of the shower slid open. She'd removed the wrap on her leg and my eyes took in the bruising that covered her calf. Her hands found and delicately ran over my shoulders and upper back.

Emotion flooded me as I wrapped my arms around her waist and buried my face against her flat belly. My back was growing cold as her body blocked the stream of water, but I wasn't about to move. I heard the squirt of shampoo and then her hands were in my hair. I nearly fell asleep as she massaged my scalp, washing my hair. She reached up and pulled down the detachable showerhead and rinsed the soap from my hair.

When she was done, I leaned back against the wall and stared up at her. She smiled softly as she began washing her own long locks. I took advantage of every second and devoured her body, cementing it to my memory. Thoughts of her belly swelling enthralled me. I wondered, not really caring, how her body would change and prayed this pregnancy would be successful and easy on her.

Des shifted on her feet and winced in pain. I gripped her hips and steadied her. "You shouldn't be standing for so long. I don't think this is what the doctor had in mind."

"I know, but I needed a shower and I couldn't resist joining you."

I pulled her to my lap and held her close. "We should get you out of here. You need to rest."

Her stomach growled loudly as she chuckled, "I don't know. I think rest needs to wait." Smiling at me she said, "Your babies are hungry."

"Mmm. I have something else that's hungry." She wiggled her bum against my erection and kissed me.

~ DESIREE ~

~ CHAPTER 25 ~

The kiss soon became heated and my body began fighting with itself. I'd missed him terribly the week I was away from him, more than I wanted to admit to anyone. I'd wronged him terribly and while it seemed he'd forgiven me, I wasn't sure I could forgive myself. His hands roamed, almost cautiously, over my back as I traced my fingers over the stubble on his jaw.

So badly I wanted to give myself over to him in the shower, but part of me wasn't in it. If O had taught me anything it was to be true to myself. Pulling back from his kiss, I placed my forehead on his and sighed before wrapping my arms around his neck.

Muffled, I whispered, "I'm so sorry, O."

Shushing me, he assured me it was ok. "Baby, let's not talk about this now. I agree that we need to talk, but I just got you back. We have all the time in the world."

I was grateful for the reprieve, but I also worried that not talking about it would grow and fester into something horrible between us. "Just promise me we'll talk, soon."

"Promise." My stomach grumbled again as he grinned at me.

Climbing off his lap, I ended our would-be tryst, "Come on. We need food."

Stepping out of the shower, I swathed a towel around my body and hobbled to the side of the tub. The pain was increasing, letting me know it was time to take it easy. Drying my leg, I then wrapped it before putting the walking cast back on. After turning the water off, O sat on the chair outside the shower and did much the same task; drying his leg before putting his prosthetic back on.

"We're quite the pair."

He agreed with a wink and added, "The perfect pair."

After we got dressed we headed to the kitchen for some breakfast. He insisted I sit down while he cooked for me. I loved watching him do his thing and I couldn't wipe the smile off my face thinking of that first morning together—and the night before on the couch.

"What are you smiling at?"

"Nothing."

Flexing his arms, with a spatula in one hand, he teased, "You call this nothing?"

Shrugging my shoulders, I egged him on. "Ehhh. I've seen better."

Dropping the spatula, he marched over to me and started tickling me, "You take that back." My hands tried restraining his as I laughed and tried wriggling out of his arms. "You give?" He stopped his torture and looked in my eyes, asking what he already knew the answer to. "I'm the best you've ever seen. Admit it."

Shaking my head and trying to control my laughter, I confessed, "You're the best I've ever *had*…in so many ways."

He stood up tall and beat his chest. "That's what I thought!" The smell of burnt pancakes began to fill the air as he rushed back over to the stove. "Dammit."

Sighing, "I may need to retract my statement." He held up the black pancake as I laughed, "I'm not eating that!"

"Ehh, syrup fixes everything."

That peaked my interest as I pursed my lips at him, curiosity getting the better of me. "Syrup, huh? I've never tried syrup." He caught my innuendo as I flashed my eyes to the bedroom.

"Noted Mrs. Kerrigan. Lucky for you the bottle is nearly full."

I devoured more pancakes than I ever had before. Finally it seemed my appetite was making an appearance. Then the fatigue set in. I remembered the first trimester exhaustion well, but this time it was so much worse. It had to be because it was twins. Covering my yawn with my hand, O rubbed a hand on my thigh.

"Babe, are you tired?"

Resting my head on his shoulder, "Exhausted. I know I shouldn't be, but...it takes a lot out of you." He questioned what 'it' was and I replied, "Pregnancy, twins."

"Get some rest then. Listen to your body." He stood and wrapped his arm around my waist. "Come on. Time for a nap!"

He tucked me under the covers and lowered his mouth to mine for a slow, soft kiss. My eyes were already heavy as he stroked my face. Kissing my cheeks, nose and chin, I felt his weight leave the bed, but couldn't even open my eyes to watch him leave the room. Hell, I think I was asleep before he made it to the bedroom door.

When I woke, I realized I'd slept for a few hours. This was so unlike me. Rolling out of bed, I found O on the couch. *Was he reading a book?* I walked up behind him to see he was reading a pregnancy book and next to him was a pile of books, some about twins.

He jumped when he heard my cast scuffing across the floor. Grinning, he admitted, "Busted."

"Where did you get these?" He pulled me down onto his lap, setting the book aside. I grabbed one and flipped it over to read the back cover.

"I ran to the bookstore down the street while you were napping." Looking at the books, he asked, "I hope that's ok."

Smiling, "It's totally ok. Did you learn anything you didn't already know?"

Snorting, he revealed, "I think the question should be 'Is there anything I knew *before* reading it?'" We both laughed. "Seriously, this is so informative. I had no idea, and twins. It's just unimaginable."

"Hmm. Well," I set the book back down, "don't mind me if I don't get too invested yet. It's just hard for me."

"I think I understand. I'm so sorry you had to go through that." We snuggled close as he asked, "Do you want to talk about it? You know you can always talk to me."

Shrugging my shoulders, "I know I should, but it happened so long ago...Some women can just brush it aside, but I've never been one of them. I'll always wonder what they would've looked like, boy or girl, what they would've grown up to be. I don't know..."

"I think that's perfectly fine." He made it a point to set his eyes on mine. "You'll be an amazing mom."

"Maybe, if it happens."

He wiped at the tear falling from my eye before I could. "It'll happen. Have faith, baby."

O kissed me and this time it stirred the feelings of desire deep inside me like it normally did. He took his time like he was memorizing every curve of my lips. Holding his face I pulled him closer as waves of passion flooded me. His hand ran over my hip and down my thigh as I pressed my tender breasts closer to him.

He lay me back on the couch and covered me with his body. "I've missed you so much. I didn't think it was possible to miss someone so much." His tongue caressed mine as I welcomed its invasion.

Softly panting, I whispered, "I missed you, too." We kissed a little while longer before I pleaded with him, "Take me to the bedroom, Odysseus."

Grunting, he climbed off of me and the couch, pulling me to my feet. Without objection, he swooped me up in his arms and carried me to the bedroom. Setting me on the bed, he fiddled with his phone and put some music on. Once he was standing in front of me again, he pulled me back to my feet and cupped the back of my neck, before kissing along my jaw.

The goosebumps and tremors were running over me as I smiled and then bit my lip, trying to make myself stand still and enjoy the attention he was lavishing on me. Slowly, his hands moved down my body and under the hem of my shirt. His eyes looked to mine asking for permission and I raised my arms as consent.

Fingering the satin of my bra, he bent to kiss the swells of my breasts. Pulling one free, he pulled my nipple into his mouth and I cried out in pleasure and pain. He released it immediately as I objected.

"Don't stop, they're just sensitive." Moaning, he freed the other and bathed it with his tongue. My panties were soaked as I tried pushing his head lower. "O, I need you." I don't think I'd ever felt so wanton in my life.

Sitting me back down, he removed my walking cast as I fully removed my bra. His hands ran under the backs of my thighs and up to cup my ass. Lifting my hips, he pulled the shorts and panties from my body in one fluid motion. Then his hand dipped between my legs and I leaned my head back further as my hips lifted into his hand.

~ ODYSSEUS ~

~ CHAPTER 26 ~

Her anticipation of my touch was one of the hottest things. Her body nearly trembling as it sought out more of my touch. I pressed her hips back down to the bed as she moaned. I stood and removed my own clothing as she watched intently. Naked before her, only the bandage on my arm, she held her arms out to me like she was welcoming me home.

With my good leg between her thighs, I ran my hand up and down her leg as she wrapped it around my waist. Her hand reached out and stroked me. Sucking in my breath, my hips bucked as I fucked her hand. I couldn't avoid her any longer. Bruising her lips, I took possession of her mouth, claiming what was mine.

Sucking and pulling on her lips, I didn't stop until she cried out, "O, please take me."

I pinned her hands above her head as I watched her will give away in an indescribable way. It'd only happened a few times since we'd been together and I don't remember anything like it ever happening with anyone else. Her eyes would roll back and when they reopened this glaze covered them. Her body became pliable and open to anything I gave it. She described it as almost like she was having an out of body experience and it was addicting to partake in.

My fingers found her dripping and open for me, right before I touched my head against her and slid in. The gasp and moan that escaped her mouth traveled through me like hot chocolate on a cold day. I buried myself in her as our fingers twisted together above her head. I pumped in and out of her for several minutes, but her orgasm surprised us both when it claimed her.

"O!" Like a crazed woman she screamed at me, pleading, "Don't stop. Odysseus!" Releasing her hands, her fingers dug into my shoulders as her hips stiffened against mine. I slowed my pace, knowing she'd be sensitive, but she encouraged me on. "No, don't stop. Give me all of you. Please, I need all of you."

Her hands gripped my ass as I pushed into her even harder. She began moaning again, "Are you close, again?" Eyes closed, she simply nodded. Arching up, I growled out, "Touch yourself."

Without hesitation, she licked two fingers and she began circling her clit. "O." She was whimpering as I dropped my head to suck on her tits.

"Tell me when, Des!"

She increased her speed and soon panted, "Now, O. NOW!"

I spilled into her, my body giving out as our sweat slick bodies clung to each other. Her cries filled my ears and then I realized they were real cries. Jerking my head up, I cupped her face, "Des, baby, what's wrong? Did I hurt you?"

She just shook her head, "I can't lose you, O. I almost lost you..."

"Hey...shh. I'm not going anywhere." I rolled to my side as she took her rightful spot on my chest. Shawn Hook's *Sound Of Your Heart* was playing as I held her close, assuring her she wasn't going to lose me. "Des, my feelings for you aren't fickle, they're life-altering. I'm in this until God takes me home and even then, I'll fight the angels or the Devil himself to get back to you."

"You should hate me, hate what I did. I was so worried things would be different between us. Your body speaks to my heart, my soul, like no other."

"I never said I didn't hate what you did. While I understood, it nearly destroyed me when I couldn't find you." She sobbed some more, clutching to my side. Trying to lighten the mood I joked, "I just think you're hormonal." She punched me in the gut as I groaned, "Ow! Guess I deserved that."

"I'm not hormonal, not on purpose anyway. And it's *your* fault. You did this to me!"

"Um, I wasn't there alone, Des."

Sighing, she pinched my nipple saying, "You're infuriating."

"You love it." I lifted her face to mine and kissed her nose. "I love you Des Kerrigan. Nothing can change that."

"Say it again."

"What, nothing can change that?"

Grinning, "No, the name part."

"Hmm, like that name do you? I like it too. It lets everyone know that you belong to me. Desiree Kerrigan."

"Even without your name, everyone knows I belong to you. I love you, Odysseus Kerrigan."

"You're sure I didn't hurt you, or the babies?"

She let out a full belly laugh as she inquired, "Didn't get that far in the book did you? You're not *that* big O."

"Hey!"

Squeezing my cock her sultry voice consumed me, "But if you were any bigger we'd definitely have a problem."

A couple hours later we emerged from the bedroom and found Will nose first in a book. One of the twin books. *Shit!* I tried snatching it from him, but he was quicker than me. He tilted his head at me and then at Des and his eyes traveled to her stomach.

"Are you, I mean... Twins?"

I scrubbed my hands over my face and looked to Des. She walked to my side and curled into me, confirming, "Yes. It's twins."

"H-O-L-Y S-H-I-T!" He exaggerated every syllable as he said it. Setting the book down, he asked, "Have you told mom and dad?"

"No. And you'll keep hush about it. We're planning to tell everyone, in our own time."

Will grinned like a fool, "How much is it worth to you?"

Des interjected, "Knock it off, Will or I'll tell everyone what you told me in the hospital." Will glared at her as I was lost and had no clue what Will had told her in the hospital. "Don't test me, Will. I'm a woman and I'm hormonal."

Scoffing, I asked, "How come you can say you're hormonal, but I can't?" She smacked my chest as I laughed.

Will agreed to keep our secret and when Des was out of the room I filled him in on her birthday surprise. Everyone was meeting us at a restaurant that Saturday night to celebrate her birthday, only Des didn't know. Her birthday had come and gone while she was in the hospital and I wanted her to know we hadn't forgotten. She hadn't said a word about it, but she deserved a night out. Everyone would be there and then some.

That Saturday afternoon I told her to get dressed. "I'm taking you to dinner." She glanced at me like she was surprised. "I made reservations and everything. We leave in two hours."

"I thought you said dinner?"

"I did. But first we're going to do some 'normal couple' things." I winked at her and left the room.

I took her to get ice cream, to the movies, and then drove downtown to the restaurant. Pulling up to valet, because I wasn't going to have her walk any further than necessary on that leg, she objected and I quickly silenced her. The valet slid in behind the wheel of her Challenger, a grin on his face, as I met her on the sidewalk.

"You know, it's not going to be so easy getting twins in and out of that thing."

"We've discussed this, O. Until the twins arrive, that car is my baby. You're lucky I even let you drive her." She wrapped her arms around me and kissed my chin. "Now I want food! We're starving!"

Hand in hand, we followed the hostess to the back room. As we walked through the doors, everyone yelled, "SURPRISE!" Des about jumped out of her skin, but was smiling from ear to ear.

"Oh my God. O, did you do this?"

"Yes. Happy Birthday, baby. Sorry it's late." She hugged me quickly before we were accosted with greetings from everyone there. All my brothers, parents, and a few friends showed up, Stacey, too. Soon Stacey, Lucy, and Des were sitting at the end of the table chatting it up as I sat down next to her, D on the other side of me.

"So, D, how's life?" He was my baby brother, but always stuck closest to Dorian while I was usually with Heath and Will. Sometimes I worried he got in to the same business as Dorian for the wrong reasons, but he was a grown man and seemed to be doing well for himself.

"You know. Same ole, same ole. You?"

"We're good. Enjoying a little normalcy. We haven't had much of that."

"Shit, and now you're having a kid. Enjoy it while you can."

Clapping his back, "I plan to! You should try it."

Laughing he grimaced, "Not likely."

~ DESIREE ~

~ CHAPTER 27 ~

"How is it that we never met until a few months ago?" Lucy and I stared at Stacey and she just laughed.

"You two have both been invited to the same things, but schedules never worked out." Stacey looked to me and said, "Don't think you're stealing my best friend. She's mine."

Lucy laughed as I teased, "We'll see about that. We're related now."

"By injection only!" Lucy and I started cracking up at Stacey's comment.

"Yes, speaking of injections..." I stood up and once O realized I was trying to get everyone's attention, he walked up behind me. He whistled and then all eyes were on me. His hands were on my shoulders as I thanked everyone.

"Thank you so, so much for being here. It means a lot to me that you've all welcomed me into your family." My damn hormones started raging as my voice cracked. "I know it hasn't been easy and it's been a whirlwind." Looking to Will, "And some of you, well, two of you, have even taken a bullet for me. It really means more than you know." O stood behind me, his chin against my temple as his arms circled in front of me. He was rubbing my belly, though I wasn't sure if he knew he was doing it. "Without the support of all of you, we wouldn't be here today."

I looked to O, and he knew what I was thinking. Whispering, "Go ahead."

"So, I'm pretty sure you all know that the whirlwind continues. It's early and I've had miscarriages in the past, so I'm hesitant to share, but we're pregnant." O squeezed my hand as the cheers began.

"Hang on, she's not done."

Everyone quieted again as I glanced to his mother, then Lucy and Heath, to Will, and back to his mother and father. "Well, I guess the family tradition continues. It's early and I'm scared to death, but come January, or sooner, there'll be another set of twins in the family."

The room grew silent and then his mother stood up asking, "Are you serious?"

O replied, "As a heart attack!"

Will threw his fist in the air, "Booyah! And I knew before all of you!"

His mother squealed and then ran over and embraced us. "I'm so happy for you."

Everyone started congratulating us and began asking how I was feeling, fluttering around me like I was a delicate flower. O joined his brothers for a celebratory shot as the girls decided to order dessert.

"So, January?" Lucy caught my attention as all eyes were on me as we ate our dessert.

"Yes, the 15th, but with it being twins, it's likely to be around Christmas."

"Aww, that's so exciting. I'm happy for you."

"Just pray for me. I'm really scared. We debated about telling anyone because I had three miscarriages several years ago. But I'd rather have everyone's support instead of going through it alone."

His mother clasped her hand over mine, "I believe everything is going to be fine. Have faith, dear." Leaning in she confessed, her voice soft so only I could hear, "I had my share of miscarriages and loss, too. D was a twin."

Glancing down the table to the youngest Kerrigan, my heart went out to them both. No one seemed to hear as I looked to her, confused. "I had no idea. I'm so sorry." I wasn't sure if she was implying that she'd lost his twin during pregnancy or after delivery and I didn't even know if anyone else knew. "Do they know?"

"They know, but D doesn't like to talk about it. He was older when it happened. It nearly tore our family apart. That's also around the time Dorian and D became inseparable. Dorian was so afraid of losing D, that he never let him out of his sight." I wiped at a stray tear. "It's ok, dear. It's been a long time. The heart can heal, but the scars still linger and ache."

"I'm sorry. O never said anything. I had no idea."

"It's ok. So, when do you find out what you're having?"

Sighing, "Uh, usually twenty weeks, I'm about eight weeks. Right now I'm just trying to make it to the second trimester."

"Set small goals. Sometimes that's best. If you need anything you just let me know."

"Thank you. I'm sure I'll be calling you all frantic at some point."

"I'm always here."

The next morning, after a bout of morning sickness, I found O still asleep in bed. There came some banging on the door to the apartment, so I wobbled my way to the door just as Will stepped from his bedroom with no shirt on. I rolled my eyes at him before looking through the peephole, and saw Detective Rollins. *What was he doing here, on a Sunday morning no less?*

Opening the door, he flashed his badge, "Desiree Kerrigan."

"Yes?"

He nodded and two other officers pushed their way around him. "Desiree Kerrigan, you're under arrest for the murder of Saul Templeton." I didn't hear anything else that they said.

Will rushed over, yelling, as Detective Rollins kept him at bay. O then burst out of the bedroom, fury covering his face once he saw what was happening.

"What the fuck are you doing?"

"Odysseus, I suggest you call an attorney. She's going to need one."

"She's pregnant! You can't lock her up."

The detective looked to me and nodded his head, "So you lied to us. You swore you weren't pregnant."

"Because you never would've let me be the bait."

"I suggest you stop talking Mrs. Kerrigan."

They started pushing me out the door, my walking cast slowing me down. "O?"

"I'll get you out of this baby. Don't say a word." He got nose to nose with the detective and spit out, "If so much as a hair is missing from her head I'll sue you and your whole department. She's pregnant with twins and has a broken leg. So help me God."

"Call your attorney. She's going to need it."

Walking out the back door, a police car was waiting as they slid me into the backseat. I became numb, not even able to cry. I was booked once we arrived at the station. I'd felt less violated by Saul and that was saying a lot. I was put in a solitary cell and given a single blanket for comfort. With it being Sunday I already knew I'd be stuck here until morning. I didn't sleep more than an hour or two that night.

The next morning I was put in an interrogation room and waited. A man in his forties, wearing an expensive suit was sent in and he sat down across from me. I wasn't sure if he was a detective or a lawyer. Watching as he pulled out some folders, a few pens, a tape recorder, and a pad of paper, I was leaning toward lawyer.

"Mrs. Kerrigan. I'm Zach Connors. Your husband hired me." I scrutinized him with my eyes knowing that there was no way O could afford him. "I'm also a good friend of Dorian's."

That made more sense. It seemed Dorian's connections were never-ending. I'd heard about Judd and how they'd come to the safe house just hours after I'd snuck out. I joked with O about making sure to never piss off Dorian because he probably knew a hitman, too.

"May I call you Desiree?"

"Des is fine."

"Ok, Des. Why don't we start from the beginning? I need to know everything about your relationship with Saul Templeton."

"I don't understand. I killed him in self-defense."

"Well, they're saying it was premeditated since you left the safe house alone and armed with a gun."

"They knew I had the gun."

"That may be, but the autopsy is saying he was shot at point blank range, almost execution style, multiple times after you tortured him."

I started laughing. "After *I* tortured *him*? Christ. What the hell is wrong with these people?"

"Des, I've spoken in great length with your husband. I know about the PPO and the attacks from Saul. All of this will play very well for you. Now, let's start from the beginning."

I told him everything. I'd met Saul through work, he was a patient. It quickly turned romantic and then I was living with him. He doted on me and vice versa. Shortly into our relationship I became pregnant to miscarry shortly after. That was around the time he started becoming very possessive and controlling. After two more miscarriages the abuse started, mostly mental and emotional before it turned into sexual abuse. I began missing work and stopped seeing my friends; friends that to this day were still out of the picture for the most part. When I tried ending things, it got ugly. I left with the help of Stacey, filed a PPO, and found a new place. I had to start from scratch with only the clothes on my back.

"He violated the PPO a few times before I started reporting it. I never thought the law wouldn't be able to protect me or that he'd take it as far as he did."

"This is all great. Now. That night. What happened?"

~ ODYSSEUS ~

~ CHAPTER 28 ~

It was Monday morning. I hadn't gotten any sleep the night before. Will sat with me at the police station, but I never did get in to see Des. Dorian and I stayed in touch via text and he said that his attorney friend wouldn't be able to do anything until morning. He was in there with her now. I was so fucking angry about her being locked up that I was ready to wring someone's neck. After all the shit Saul had put her through, the department's lack of protecting her, and she finally did what needed to be done, and now they were arresting her for his murder. What she did to him couldn't be justified as murder, it was mercy. If I'd gotten my hands on him, *that* would've been murder.

I didn't get a chance to see her until we sat in front of the judge. It took all my willpower not to jump over the seats and hug her. She had bags under her eyes, but put on a brave smile. The judge was talking and I tried to focus.

"How does the defendant plea?"

"Not guilty, your Honor."

"Bond?"

"We'd like the defendant retained in custody. She's a doctor and has connections."

"Your Honor, exactly. She's a doctor and has patients to care for. She has a broken leg and is pregnant. She's not going anywhere. We ask that she be released to her own recognizance."

My blood was boiling.

"Bail is set at one hundred thousand."

Jesus fuck. Where the hell was I going to get that kind of money? They dragged her away before I could say two words to her. The attorney motioned to me and I stepped closer.

"This is all normal. Do you have anyone who can post bail?" I just shook my head. I couldn't ask anyone to do that for us.

"It's already taken care of." I turned to stare at Dorian. Where had he come from? "Don't worry. We got you covered."

About an hour later, I waited in the station for her to be released. Dorian, Heath, and Will had put up the gyms and the apartments as collateral for bail. I would never be able to repay them for their belief in us. Des emerged from the back and walked toward me. Closing my eyes, I sighed as I held her.

She seemed completely detached as she mumbled, "Please get me out of here."

We walked out to my truck and I helped her climb in. Once I sat next to her, I wrapped my arms around her, but she didn't return the sentiment. "Des?" She pulled back when I tried to stroke her cheek.

"O, please. I just want to go home."

I couldn't keep my mouth shut. "I would've kept you safe, Des."

She glared at me, knowing what I was referring to. "I know, but it was the only way I knew how to keep *you* safe."

Sighing, I kissed her hand. "You're infuriating. But I still love you."

With half a smile, she replied, "Just the way you like it."

She fell asleep on the way home and woke as I opened up her door. "Did you sleep at all?"

"What do you think?" She was pissy and I understood, I just wish she wouldn't take it out on me.

She walked right into the bedroom and sat on the bed. "Can I draw you a bath?"

"Hmm?"

"A bath. I'm going to fill the tub."

"I can't." She pointed at her leg. "I'm not supposed to soak it."

"We'll prop it up." She just nodded as I walked to the bathroom and filled the tub.

She didn't talk, just lay back in the tub. I was surprised she let me wash her body, but it was almost like she wasn't aware of it. I took care to keep her leg dry. Washing her hair, I could see the fatigue claiming her. Once her hair was rinsed, I pulled the plug and helped her to her feet. Wrapping a towel around her once she stepped from the tub, I carried her to the bedroom.

Pulling a t-shirt and underwear from her drawer, I helped her dress. "Can I get you anything?"

"Some juice or fruit would be nice."

I kissed her temple and left for the kitchen. I returned with a glass of apple juice and some fresh fruit to find her passed out. Pulling the covers over her, I placed the juice and fruit on the night stand. I sat down on the other side of the bed, my head against the headboard. What the hell were we going to do now? Every time we thought everything was fine, something horrible would happen.

I wanted to believe her attorney, that this wouldn't last long and if it did that no jury would find her guilty. He said that he was waiting for a plea bargain from the DA. I told him there was no way she was serving time for protecting herself.

The next morning Des got a phone call from work. They needed her to come in, but wouldn't tell her why. We drove in silence to her office, but she insisted I wait in the car. I was leaning against the side of the car when I saw her walking back outside with a box in her hands.

Rushing over to her I questioned her, "What's going on?"

"They fired me. They can't afford to have me tarnish their record."

"It was self-defense. What the fuck?" I started to walk into the building when she grabbed my arm.

"Please, O. I already told them all of that. It's business. They can't have a murder suspect working for them."

I took the box from her and put it in the backseat. Once we were both sitting in the car and buckled up I asked, "Can you fight it?"

She shrugged her shoulders, "I don't know. Probably not until the trial is over or whatever."

I didn't know what to say. It was like I could see her slipping into a dark depression and no one could blame her. Starting the car, we drove in silence, music the only sound. *The Only Reason* by Puddle of Mudd was playing. I hoped she was listening to the words because I knew I was.

That night I was down in the gym with Will and D. Des was upstairs watching a movie and had a phone call scheduled with Zack. I was hitting the heavy bag, taking out my frustration when D walked over and offered me a bottle of water.

"You hanging in there?" I scoffed, downed some water, and attacked the bag once more after he stepped behind it. "Do you really think they'll convict her? I mean he shot you, Will, and almost killed her. This is absurd."

"I still had faith in the justice system, but now... I don't know. The whole thing is ridiculous. All the evidence on the books of what he did to her and they're charging her with murder." I put in a few more hits. "Of course she fucking blew his head off. I would've too. FUCK!" I took the gloves off and threw them aside. "I can't even think about it. What was he doing or going to do to her that night? Will battled with him and got a bullet to the gut." I was freaking out.

"Dude, breathe. She's fine, upstairs and pregnant." The look I gave him must've sent the wrong message. "Dude, they're yours right?"

"What? Jesus. Yes, they're mine." Were they mine? Fuck. I sat down on the bench and grabbed my phone. Did I worry she'd cheated on me? No. But he'd raped her right before we got together. She'd had a period. This was asinine. "Yes, of course they're mine."

"Sorry. The look you gave me."

"It was in regards to her being pregnant, in general, not me doubting her fidelity." Dropping my head to my hands I started thinking about all the financial obligations. "Fuck. She lost her job. How am I going to pay for all this?"

"O, you need to relax. You have plenty of time. Everything's going to be fine."

"We were supposed to be looking at houses. Now."

"I'm sorry. That does suck."

I groaned as I spotted Will across the gym with a client. "I don't think Will's going to be ok with two babies invading his bachelor pad."

"Yeah. Good luck with that."

"Thanks."

"Anytime." He bumped my shoulder and announced, "My turn. Hold the bag, fucker."

~ DESIREE ~

~ CHAPTER 29 ~

Independence Day was approaching. I fingered the necklace he'd given me for my birthday. It was a diamond heart pendant in white gold with an anchor in the middle. I loved it. It went with almost everything, casual or fancy. I was supposed to be packing my bags to head up to the lake house for a few nights, but I had no desire to celebrate. There was talk the trial would start soon, having turned down all the plea offers.

O walked in, "Are you ready?"

Sighing, "O, I can't go."

"Zack said it was fine. We're not leaving the state."

"That's not it. I can't do this. I can't pretend everything is fine when my world is crumbling around me. No matter how hard I try..."

He gripped my shoulders, "Stop it! You don't get to do this to me again."

"Do what?"

"Give up! I know how hard this is. Fuck." He walked away from me and smashed the mirror with his fist.

"O!" Shards fell to the dresser and on the floor as blood began to cover his hand.

Panting, he sounded broken, the way I felt. "I can't lose you Des. My nights are finally peaceful because of you. My bleak future shines bright because of you. My life has purpose because of you." I wiped at my own tears as he let his fall, baring his soul to me. "Did you know that I was so depressed, I imagined doing unthinkable things, and then I saw you for the first time?"

"Wh...what?"

"I'm not telling you this out of guilt, but because I don't think you quite understand how important you are to me. I saw you working with another patient and you just glowed. You never even noticed me, not because you didn't see me, but because you didn't see this." He lifted his prosthetic but my eyes stayed on his. "You're the only person in that place that didn't look at her patients like they were damaged goods. All you saw was the person. You gave me hope when mine had all but run out." Pulling a t-shirt out of a drawer, I wrapped it around his hand. "You can't lose hope. Hope is what made me fall in love with you."

Sniffling, "I don't know if I have any hope left, O."

With his uninjured hand, he touched the tiny bump that was forming low on my belly. "Yes, you do. You have at least two reasons to be full of hope. Baby, do you realize what next week is?" Wiping at more tears, I shook my head. "Second trimester."

My eyes searched his as I digested his words. *That couldn't be right, could it?* When I realized he was right, I wrapped my arms around his waist. We'd talked a lot. He knew I'd never made it this far, let alone into the second trimester, and we were almost there. I'd had a couple of appointments and everything always came back perfectly normal, but having faith and hope in it all was a different thing all together.

"We can stay home if you want, but I don't want us to be apart."

I shook my head. "You're right. I'm sorry." I covered his hand with my own. "I'm sorry I've been so detached. I just…"

"I get it, Des. I do. But pretending they're not a part of you isn't healthy either."

We cleaned up his hand and the glass and finished packing our bags. I slept most of the drive up, though I tried hard to stay awake. The car slowing woke me as we pulled down the long gravel drive.

"Where is everyone?"

He laughed, "I may have lied about everyone being up here. It's just us. Heath and Lucy are with her parents. We have the beach to ourselves." He was grinning from ear to ear and I couldn't help but smile too. "Think of it as a belated honeymoon."

"Honeymoon, huh?" The sun was beginning to set as I strolled right for the beach.

"Where you going?"

"I'm going swimming." I pulled my shirt off and dropped it on the back porch as he followed. "Care to join me?" Kicking my sandals off—grateful I was done with the walking cast—and stepping out of my maxi skirt, I stood on the beach in my bra and panties as I slowly backed into the water.

He followed suit and met me in the water. "I can't imagine this is good for my prosthetic."

"It'll dry. Kiss me, O."

We waded out further as the sun glowed orange and pink on the horizon, our mouths inseparable. Our hunger for each other was obvious. I'd shut him out since my arrest and it was a mistake. I needed him inside me, beside me, all around me like I needed air to breathe.

A speedboat full of people drove by and honked the horn as they cheered us on. Pulling away from him, I buried my face in his chest in embarrassment. He just pulled me closer, his erection pressing against my belly as his hands cupped me through my panties.

"O." He just looked at me like he wasn't doing anything out of the ordinary. "Let's go inside."

Grinning, "Let's not. This was *your* idea, not mine." He slid his fingers under the fabric and rubbed his thumb over my sensitive flesh. My hands clutched his biceps as I tried to appear normal. "How horny are you, Des? Hmm. I wonder how quick I can get you to fall apart all around me."

"Pretty," I gasped, "quick." Lifting my head, I begged, "Kiss me."

Slowly his mouth worked over mine while his fingers moved to a quicker pace. My legs buckled as he held me up. "You're so sexy."

"Kiss me!"

"Not until you're done. How many people do you think see you and know what I'm doing to you?" I tensed as my head moved. "Don't look. You'll just draw more attention to us."

"Dammit, O. Don't stop." My head dropped to his chest as the final tremors of my orgasm burst through me. I tried to make it look like I was simply hugging him, both of us knowing it was so much more than that.

On shaky legs I walked back to the beach with O right behind me. He took me by surprise and swooped me up in his arms. I squealed and clung tight to his neck as he carried us back to the house. The door was locked so he had no choice but to set me on my feet.

"Shit." His keys were in his shorts back on the beach. "I'll be right back."

The wind was starting to pick up as I stood on the porch, shivering, and waiting for him to return. He was a gem and grabbed my discarded clothes as well. Once we got in the house I headed straight for the kitchen, famished once again. It looked like Heath and Lucy had stocked the fridge and I was eternally grateful. Fruit and veggies had already been prepped, along with a mini cheese tray that was covered in plastic wrap. Pulling it all out, O and I indulged.

"I feel grimy. I'm going to take a shower."

I headed back to the bedroom we'd stayed in weeks prior and found a wrapped gift on the bed. The card had my name on it and I opened it. It was from Lucy.

I'm so happy for you and O.
I've always wanted a sister
and part of me feels like
I finally have one.
Enjoy!
~Lucy

I managed to hold back the tears as I opened the box. O came barreling through the door with our bags from the car.

"What's that?"

"I don't know, I'm about to open it. It's from Lucy."

He dropped the bags and encouraged me, "Well, open it!"

Inside was an array of personal spa products and a coupon book. I laughed when I realized what she'd done. O picked up the coupon book and I made sure he knew that they were for me to redeem with him and not the other way around.

"What the hell? What do I get?"

Giggling, I replied, "You get to rub me down whenever I ask!"

He just grunted in response as I continued pulling items from the box. At the bottom were two onesies in Dr. Seuss themed colors. One said 'Thing 1' and the other 'Thing 2'. There were matching red and white striped pants and little hats. They were adorable and perfect. O smiled and grabbed one and held it over my belly.

"I don't know. I think they're a little big." Winking, he placed them back in the box. "Lucy spoiled you."

"I know. I love it all." Snatching the coupon book, I browsed through it and pulled a coupon out and handed it to O. "I expect this to happen once I'm out of the shower."

"As you wish." He bowed as I laughed at him.

When I got out of the shower, the bedroom was lit with candles and music was playing. I couldn't help but smile. His back was turned as I pulled the towel tight around my body. I stood and admired him as he busied himself with candles and lotions on the night stand. He was shirtless, still in nothing but his underwear from our swim. His broad shoulders always got my attention as they flexed with every movement.

Spotting me, he smiled and said, "Don't move. Two minutes." He pecked my cheek as he walked by, stripped off his boxers, and jumped in the shower.

Leaning against the bathroom door frame, I watched him quickly bathe. When he stepped out of the shower he was at half-mast. I eyed it and then him and just smiled. Grabbing a towel, he shooed me out of the bathroom and into the bedroom.

"Come here." Slowly, I walked to him as he carefully removed the towel from my body. "My mission tonight is to please you at least four times, since three is our current standing record." I started to speak, but his finger silenced me. "No debates, Des. Just you, me, and lots of pleasure."

~ ODYSSEUS ~

~ CHAPTER 30 ~

Her beauty would never wear on me. It was the exact reason I selected *Never Seen Anything Quite Like You* by The Script. Naked, clothed, hair up or down, makeup done or streaked with tears, she was the most beautiful creature I'd ever laid eyes on. Her flat belly was starting to show signs of the two lives she was growing inside her. The love and devotion I felt for her knew no bounds. I continued running my hands over her body and slowly turned her around. My hands drifted across her chest, pulling her against my front. Her head relaxed against my shoulder as I kissed the exposed flesh of her neck while her hair draped down the other side.

"Have you thought about how I should please you?" She gently shook her head. "Cuz I have. I want you riding me at least once, my cock and my face." A chill ran over her and I grinned. "I think you like that."

My hands moved down to her belly as I rubbed the curve of her expanding womb. I noticed that her breasts felt slightly larger as I gently kneaded them. Her small hands traced circles over the tops of my thighs and one grazed the side of my growing erection.

"Careful, Des."

Whining, she pleaded, "O, please."

"Patience grasshopper." She turned in my arms and buried her face in my neck as I caressed her back and the curve of her ass. Standing on her tip toes, she positioned my cock between her legs as we both moaned. "You're a minx."

"So punish me." Her words were like fire in my veins. With sternness in my voice, I demanded, "Lie down."

Des climbed on the bed in a way to make sure I could see every part of her. Up on all fours, she moved slowly to the headboard. *Temptress.* Once she was sprawled out, I sat down next to her and removed my prosthetic. All the supplies I needed on the night stand.

Grabbing the massage oil, "Front or back first."

"Front." She pulled her hair up and spread it across the pillow, fully exposing her breasts.

Squirting the oil in my hands, I started with her feet and then up each calf. Her feet were ticklish, but she was able to relax and enjoy it for the most part. Moving closer, I began my work on her thighs. Her eyes closed as she sank a little further into the bed. Leaning down, I kissed her belly and worked my mouth lower. Spreading her legs, I kissed every part but the one spot I knew she wanted my lips most.

"O!"

"Yes?"

She groaned, knowing I was going to take my time. *Connect The Dots* by The Spill Canvas was now playing, a song I'd discovered on her playlist a few weeks back. Dripping oil on her breasts and abdomen, I ran my slick hands over her. Her hips arched when I touched them and her nipples stood at attention. Running two fingers down from the center of her chest, I didn't stop until they slid all the way inside her.

Gasping, she clenched the covers and pressed into my hand. "O, please don't stop."

It was as if all the anticipation and massaging her was the ultimate foreplay. At this rate three more orgasms would be easy peasy. Hooking my fingers up, she rocked back and forth with only one mission in mind. Practically salivating, I lowered my mouth to her clit and sucked on it gently. Slowly, I lapped my tongue in circles as she fucked my hand harder, clenching around me so intensely, like I'd never felt her do before.

My eyes lifted to find her watching me as she groaned, almost animal-like. "Odysseus."

Lifting my face, I asked, "You like watching me fuck you? I love watching you watch me. Show me your O face, Des."

I dropped my face as she kept her eyes on mine. My free hand reached up and clasped hers as she bucked into my face, crying out, my name a whisper on her lips. I continued to lick her until she begged me to stop. She pulled my mouth to hers as I crawled up to lay next to her.

"That was amazing, babe."

"I'm not done with you. Roll over." She smiled and obliged. "So I believe the count is at two and it's still early. Maybe we should try for five."

Softly, she giggled and said, "Depends if you want me to be able to walk tomorrow."

"Oh, you'll be able to walk. But I want you to remember what I did to you every time you sit down tomorrow, and maybe the next day too."

"Mmm. Give me all you got, O. I can take it."

"I know you can and I love you all the more for it."

Several minutes later after massaging her back, her ass was in the air as I fucked her from behind. She was sensitive so it was easy to get her to succumb to her orgasm for a third time. My thumb pressed against her ass while her own fingers manipulated her clit as I pumped in and out of her.

"O, now!"

Her hips stiffened and her back arched as she clenched me tight. My seed shot from me as I held her still, slowly rocking in and out of her. I finally pulled out of her and I was still semi-hard. "Fuck!"

We collapsed on the bed next to one another as she gave me a questioning look. I pointed to my dick and she smiled wickedly. "Seems like your cock is ready for more, but are you?"

"I should be asking you the same question. I'll always be ready for more."

"Hmmm....I just need a short nap. Like twenty minutes."

"Deal." We lay there, catching our breath, our bodies sweat and sex covered as she curled into me, using me as her own personal pillow.

A few hours later I woke to hands and lips moving all over my body. As my eyes adjusted to the darkness, I saw Des. She spotted my open eyes and smiled, continuing her progression. Her warm tongue immediately turned my dick rock hard in her mouth. I propped my head up on my hands and let her lavish me with her attention.

A few minutes later, she sat up and lowered her chest to mine. "I want that fourth orgasm you owe me."

Grinning, "I think I can handle that. Night's not over yet."

Gripping her hips, I pulled her closer, my dick wedged between our bodies as she gently rocked against him. Her hair fanned around our faces as she kissed me. Nipples rubbed against my chest as I rubbed her back. Reaching all the way down, I ran my hand over her sex from behind, causing her to gasp. Sitting up, she took hold of my dick and slid down my length, her eyes fluttering as she did so.

"Christ, Des. I could get used to waking up this way." She just moaned in response as she continued to lube my dick with her juices.

Up and down in short strokes until I was fully sheathed inside her, her hands rested flat on my six pack as she began riding me. My hands couldn't decide what part of her to touch, so I touched every part I could reach. Her tits, her belly, back, ribcage, hips, thighs, I even gathered her hair and tugged. She moved in a figure eight, then side to side and back to front.

"O, I don't want to stop. You feel so good." She brought her panting mouth down to mine as I became consumed in our kiss.

"Fuck me, Des. Hard."

Whimpering from pleasure, she grabbed hold of the headboard and did just as I asked. My hips thrust up to meet her as that glaze of hers appeared. Her mouth was parted as she mewled obscenities and fucked me harder.

"O, help me. I want to come."

"What do you want? Tell me what to do. I want you to come on me, Des."

Leaning back, her clit was now exposed and I immediately tended to it. "Yes, don't stop." She arched back further and the pressure on my cock nearly killed me—in a good way. "O!"

I sat up, continuing to stroke her as she clung to my body, shaking and shivering all around me. "Des, don't stop."

"Fuck me, O."

She was still coming down from her own orgasm as I flipped her to her back. Throwing a leg over my shoulder, I gave her everything I had as she ran soothing circles over her clit. I couldn't hold it in any longer and collapsing on top of her, I gave her every last drop.

"I love you, O. Thank you."

"For what?"

"For never giving up, for always loving me even when I know I made it impossible."

"You're my heart Des. You've captivated me body, heart and soul. I didn't have a choice in the matter." I kissed her as I stroked her face. "I should be thanking you. You gave me the most amazing gift when you gave me your heart, your trust, your vow, your acceptance." Rolling to my side because I was growing worried I'd crush her and the babies, I pulled her close.

With her head on my shoulder, she positioned herself on her back. Her hand started circling her belly. In the last twelve hours I'd seen her rub her belly more than I had since we found out. Her detachment from them after all the loss made sense to me, but I didn't want her to regret not loving every little piece of them if God forbid something did happen. I knew she loved them even if she was scared to admit it.

~ DESIREE ~

~ CHAPTER 31 ~

We lay in bed and talked for a while and then, O with his head on my belly, started talking to it.

"Hello babies. This is your daddy." I couldn't help but chuckle at him. It was so sweet. "Your mommy is the most beautiful woman around. If you're boys, you have to help me keep her safe. And if you're girls, then Lord help me. Your uncles and I will be fighting off the boys with baseball bats."

"What if it's a boy *and* a girl?"

"Well, I hadn't thought about that. I guess that means the boy and I can both protect our ladies." He moved up and placed his head next to mine on the pillow. "Have you thought about what they might be, Des? Any mommy intuition going on?"

I pursed my lips and shook my head. "I'm just praying for healthy. That's all I want. What about you?"

He sighed, "Well now I sound all selfish. I mean, all I know is boys so part of me hopes for boys, but a mini Des walking around sounds pretty incredible too. I guess one of each would be the perfect solution."

"What if I told you I didn't want to know the sex?"

"What?" I laughed at his reaction. "You mean, like not find out till they're born." I nodded. "You're out of your damn mind. If it's girls you're going to want everything in pink and if they're boys, blue."

"I don't know. This whole thing has been one big surprise after another. I just figured we'd continue the streak."

He rolled to his back and brought me with him. "I have to think about this. But it sounds like crazy talk."

Pinching his nipples, I cackled, "I'm not crazy!"

"Hey now," he was trying to pin my arms to my side, "if your nipples are off limits then so are mine!"

"I didn't say mine were off limits, I said they're very tender and to be careful."

He flipped me to my back, pinning my body with his. "In that case," he sucked one into his mouth as I moaned, "I'll be *very* careful."

In the late morning we both finally woke from our slumber. Something was making noise but I couldn't quite figure out what it was. Finally it dawned on me. It was my cell phone. Dread washed over me.

"O, where's my bag?"

"Hmm?"

"O, get up!" He was draped on me and it was all I could do to move him off of me. "O! My phone."

"Shit!" He jumped up and fell off the bed, forgetting his prosthetic wasn't on. "Fucking, dammit."

I curled my lips in and around my teeth, trying to not laugh. "Are you ok?"

Sneering at me as he pulled himself back up to the bed, he growled, "You can wipe that fucking grin off your face." I just stared back at him as he smiled.

The laugh burst from my lungs as I tried apologizing. "Oh, my God. If you saw what I did. Your white ass up and then flopping in the air as you toppled over."

"Alright. Keep laughing about it. I'll make you pay." He was teasing me and was in good spirits as we continued to rib each other. Then my phone began ringing again. "Shit. Your purse is over there."

He pointed to where the bags were and I jumped off the bed and began digging through my purse. I was right to be worried. It was Zack, my attorney. "It's Zack."

O motioned me to sit down next to him and spit out, "Well, answer it."

Sitting down, I took a deep breath, "Zack. Yes, we're both here. Hang on." He had me put it on speaker. This couldn't be good. "Ok, you're on speaker."

O clutched my hand as Zack's voice droned over the speaker. "I hope you're sitting down. They dropped it." We were both silent, I know I hadn't heard him right. "Are you there? Des, O?"

O chimed in, "I'm sorry, can you repeat that?"

"They dropped the charges. I don't know who your fairy godmother is, but she's working her magic. They also found out who was helping him. That doctor you mentioned he once had a thing with, I think they were partners. I digress, I was confident you wouldn't be convicted, but I didn't think they'd give up so easy. Anyway. Enjoy your holiday. You're free to fly to Antarctica if you want."

"Thank you, Zack. Same to you." O ended the call and looked to me.

I burst into tears. "Is this a joke? Please tell me I'm not dreaming."

He wrapped me in his arms, "I knew this couldn't last. Oh my, God. I love you baby. So much." He pulled my hands from my face and wiped my tears. "You're free, Des."

"You have no idea." I threw my arms around his neck. It was over, finally. I still couldn't believe it, but I was overjoyed. "Can we go shopping?"

"Shopping?"

I nodded, "Yes. I'd like to go shopping for baby clothes. Maybe open a registry."

He grinned like a fool from ear to ear. "Absofuckinglutely!"

Hope bloomed inside me and for once I felt free. Saul was gone. I wasn't going to jail and I was pregnant with twins. I looked to the man I loved as we drove down the freeway. How had I become so lucky? I'd tried leaving him behind more than once, this person I was still getting to know and I knew I was a fool. I let him drive with the agreement I could pick the music. *Wait* by Sarah McLachlan played and her lyrics tugged at my heart. We'd almost lost so much and still had so much to gain. I rubbed my belly and closed my eyes and reflected.

When someone you barely know touches a part of your soul that has been lying dormant for so long that you forgot it existed; how do you walk away from them? How do you let them go? There's only one answer. You can't, you don't, you won't. Love knows no bounds, no age, no time frame.

We ended up spending a few more days than anticipated up at the lake house. Heath and Lucy came home and we enjoyed the extra time with them. That night the four of us sat on the beach enjoying S'mores and fireworks. It was an amazing getaway and everything we needed.

Sitting on the deck, Heath looked to us and started talking. "So, Will and I have been talking. We wanted to run something by you two." We nodded our heads, not sure what was coming. "We feel there's a need for the gym to have a Physical Therapist on staff. We have a lot of soldiers, especially up here, and want to know your thoughts."

I was speechless and O was smiling, seemingly speechless as well. "I, uh, I'm pregnant with twins, Heath. I don't know what to say."

"You're pregnant, not disabled." O grinned at his own statement, "Right, that's me." I smacked his shoulder. "Babe, this could be perfect for you. You could make your own hours, etc. We could work together."

"Uh, I believe I gave you my opinion of couples who work together when we first started dating." I ran my hands through my hair and looked to each of them. "The gym up here? We don't have a place to live."

Lucy perked up, "Actually... We just put an offer on a place and it was accepted. You guys can stay here."

"What do you mean we can stay here?" O asked what I was wondering.

"It's taken care of. Mom and dad already agreed. They're willing to sell you the house. They just want permission to come visit the babies whenever possible."

My brain was on overload. I didn't know what to say or think. "I'm so honored. I don't know what to say. Can I sleep on it?"

"Of course you can."

Curiosity had me asking, "Where's the place you're buying?"

Lucy started clapping and chirped, "Two doors that way!"

"Seriously?"

"Seriously!"

"That's amazing. We'd be neighbors."

Heath grinned at Lucy and me both before teasing me. "Keep it up, Lucy. I think we have her sold. Just think Des, you'd have Lucy right down the road and once those babies are born, mom will probably move in."

Scoffing, I said, "I love your mother, but she's not living here." Heath and O just laughed like I missed the joke. "What's so funny?"

Lucy chimed in, "She's great. And with twins, take all the help you can get!"

"This is true. There's a lot that we'd have to do with licensing."

"Will and I have already started looking into it."

"Efficient aren't you?" I exhaled sharply, "Ok. O and I need to talk about it, but I'm so honored. I think it's a great idea. Veterans need more access to PT and if that means they get it at a gym, then so be it." O squeezed my hand and I smiled back at him.

~ ODYSSEUS ~

~ CHAPTER 32 ~

The next few months passed without a single problem. Des was dealing with morning sickness still, but other than that she was complication free, besides it being a multiple pregnancy. We knew what we were having—I'd convinced Des we should find out—but we hadn't told anyone. We were enjoying torturing them.

Heath and Lucy had moved into their house and we'd moved into my parents' lake house. It was weird and surreal and an amazing blessing. We entered into an agreement with my parents to buy the place after many discussions with them and Heath and Lucy. Des had been worried that Heath and Lucy would feel we were stepping on their toes. They gave us their blessing, insisting they didn't want the place. We could never expect such a nice place for our first home. Living on the water scared Des, but I promised we'd teach the twins to swim from birth.

That Halloween, everyone was headed up to celebrate. I found Des staring at the baby registry again. She had another window open, staring at car seats in neutral and not so neutral colors.

"Babe," I pointed at one, "you want that one? Let's just tell everyone and then you can get exactly what you want."

Sighing, "The shower's only a month away."

"Exactly. We can tell everyone this weekend. Have one of those gender reveals or whatever you call them."

I watched as she mulled it over. I knew it was killing her keeping it a secret. Rubbing my hands over her protruding belly, I whispered, "Come on, convince mommy to tell everyone." They kicked back and we laughed.

"Ok. BUT, the names are secret. We're not telling anyone their names until they're born. I want something just for you and me."

Sticking my hand out we shook on it. "Deal. And we're not 100% agreed on names yet."

"My vagina says that we are!"

I glared at her and we both started cracking up. "How is your vagina? Needing any attention?"

"Play your cards right, Mr. Kerrigan..."

That weekend the whole gang gathered in the kitchen and living room. D and Dorian were flying solo as usual and Will had some floozy with him that Lucy and Des immediately disliked. Des and Lucy spent all day getting the house ready. Everyone brought us housewarming gifts as well which was unexpected but appreciated.

"Ok, everyone." All eyes turned to Des and me as we stood in the kitchen. "What you don't know is that Des and I have decided to reveal the genders of the twins to you all tonight." Everyone cheered. "We just really want you all to know how grateful we are for all of you."

"Yeah, yeah. Get to the gender reveal!" Everyone laughed at my mom's demand. She was chomping at the bit to know.

"Calm your jets, Mom!"

I headed toward the back deck and everyone followed. We'd hung up a piñata filled with candy and a box filled with balloons. Each revealing the gender of one of the twins.

"Ok, so the piñata is filled with colored confetti, pink or blue, and the box with balloons. The box is for twin B and the piñata for twin A. Mom, you want the honors?"

She squealed and ran to the box as everyone gathered around. As she pried it open, pink balloons flooded the sky. "A girl? Really?" We nodded. "Finally, a girl!" She hugged us both as everyone cheered.

I offered the bat to my dad and he passed. "Shit, I took a bullet for them. Give me that." Will snatched the bat and everyone stood back as he took aim of the piñata. He managed to put a good dent in it with the first hit, but hit two had confetti scattering everywhere.

My mom gasped, "No?" Des was in tears she was so happy and my mom followed suit. "Two girls. I can't wait!"

"And they're fraternal so we'll be able to tell them apart...we hope!"

Everyone took their turn congratulating us as we fielded more questions. "Do you have names picked out?"

Des interjected, "Yes, we do. But we're not telling. That's something you'll have to wait for."

My mom pouted but took Des' answer as final.

Thanksgiving came as we celebrated Heath and Lucy's two year anniversary a little early and we had the baby shower for Des and the girls. Our friends and family were beyond generous. We got both cribs, car seats, a double stroller, and a shit ton of other stuff that I had no idea we needed or wanted. We sat in the nursery that night just taking it all in.

"Jesus. It looks like a bottle of Pepto Bismol threw up in here."

"Aren't you glad I didn't pick pink walls? Then it'd really be bad!"

"Thank God for originality."

Des had done an Alice in Wonderland meets Steampunk themed room. I wasn't on board with it at first, but it was coming together and looking pretty badass. She and Lucy spent almost every spare moment together in there.

"Any more news on the Lucy front?" She frowned and shook her head. "That sucks."

"I've been in her shoes. Sort of. I pray every day it'll happen for them. He's being great, but it's really hard on their relationship."

"What do you mean?"

"We were really lucky, O. They're going to doctors, having sex based on schedules, and thinking about trying fertility medications. The stress alone makes it really difficult to conceive."

"Wow. I had no idea."

"Ouch." I looked to her as she rubbed on her upper belly. "*Your* daughter is going to break my ribs."

"I see how it is. When they're hurting you they're mine, but when they're playing tag with you they're yours."

"Get used to it. *My* girls are perfect angels. *Yours*...not so much."

"Yeah, yeah. Listen. We need to make a decision about the car."

Sighing in resignation, she said, "I love that car, but it's not practical with twins."

Groaning, "I'll get rid of my truck before you get rid of that car."

Smiling, "Ohhh, I see. That's what this is about." She walked over and sat in my lap. "If you want the car, just say so."

"I hate to give up my truck, but I want that car more."

"You're going to have to kiss me for it."

Standing up, I headed toward our bedroom. "I think that can be arranged."

We had just left our last Lamaze class and were headed to my parents' for our family Christmas. It was actually about a week before Christmas, but it was what worked best for everyone. Des was getting too close to her due date for us to be messing around with family parties. Des and I had plans to enjoy our first Christmas together being lazy, knowing that next year our world would be running on the schedule of our two little miracles.

She gasped next to me and I looked to her. I watched as she tried to get comfortable. The weight of the babies was growing increasingly difficult on her, making it almost impossible for her to sleep for long stretches. I would never tell her, but it was taking its toll on her and it scared me to death. She had bags under her eyes where there never used to be any.

"You ok?"

"I don't know. Something's not right." My heart rate picked up as she closed her eyes. "I don't think this is a Braxton Hicks."

We were close to the hospital and I wasn't taking any chances. "We're going to the hospital."

"Oh, shit." She was trying to control her breathing as I turned the car around. "I think that's a good idea, but I don't have my bag."

"Fuck your bag. I'll have Lucy grab it."

A few seconds later she cried out in pain, screaming, "O! Something's wrong."

She grabbed my hand as I looked at the clock. "We're only a few minutes from the hospital. Hang on, Des."

I tried counting her contractions, if that's what they were, and grabbed my cell phone. Dialing 9-1-1, though I may have been overreacting, I wasn't willing to risk it. We were more than a few minutes from the hospital, but I couldn't tell Des that. Des seemed to be in her own world as I began talking to the operator. I gave her our location and plate number as I flew down the highway. Soon a patrol car caught up to me and got in front of me, clearing the way.

When I looked over to Des, she seemed to be passed out. "Des!" She was breathing, but she wouldn't respond to me. "Please, God, no!"

The operator called ahead to the hospital and when I flew into the emergency lot, they were waiting with a gurney. Opening her door, they pulled her out and all I saw was a puddle of blood in the seat. Jumping out of the car, I ran after them as they wheeled her inside. One nurse was straddling her and cutting her clothes away.

As we reached a set of double doors, I was held back as they began asking me questions. I told them who her doctor was, that she was almost thirty six weeks along with girls and that there had been no complications.

"I need to be with her."

"I'm sorry, but you'll have to wait. As soon as we have any news, we'll let you know."

I couldn't believe what I was about to say, but I said it. "You tell them to save her. I can't lose her." She nodded and left me in the hall.

~ DESIREE ~

~ CHAPTER 33 ~

I wasn't sure where I was, but everything was blindingly bright. I tried covering my face, but I couldn't move my arms. There were lights shining from above and a blue curtain in front of me. Faces covered in surgical masks fluttered around me and began talking to me like I couldn't hear them.

"Please, my girls. O?"

"She's coming to, get her back under."

I was certain I heard the faint cry of a newborn baby when everything went black once more. And although it went black, I swore I could still hear them talking. The cries of a baby and then another. My girls. I heard the familiar sound of suction from my days of being a med student and tried to talk, but my mouth wouldn't work.

"My girls, are my girls ok?" That was my silent plea that I tried to voice. *"O, where's O? He should be here with me."* I felt a weird tugging and heard more yelling.

"We're losing her. We need more blood."

Losing her? Who were they losing? Not one of my girls. Then the strangest thing happened. It was like I was having a celestial experience. I now stood behind the doctors, observing as they worked over my body frantically. That couldn't be my body, though. Could it?

Small cries filled my ears and drew my attention. Floating over to the two infant cribs I looked at my girls, knowing without a doubt they were mine. They were beautiful and definitely fraternal. One had a head full of dark hair just like her daddy and the other was almost entirely bald with blonde fuzz covering her head. They were perfect. I watched as they stamped their feet and then wiped them clean. Then they started pushing them out of the room.

"Wait, come back."

I looked to the woman who did look a lot like me on the table and watched as they pulled out the paddles and shocked her. I had a decision to make. Follow my girls or watch over the woman on the table. I followed my girls. When I emerged into the hall, the girls were gone. I looked frantically in both directions and ran through another door. I saw O on the floor, his hands covering his face. Why was he crying?

"O, stop crying. We're all ok." I tried to touch his shoulder, but my hand just floated through him.

His head jerked up as he looked toward me. A nurse appeared and started talking to him. Jumping to his feet as fast as his prosthetic would allow, he ran down the hall after the nurse. Following them, they disappeared too quickly. I ended up back in the room where they were still working over the woman who could pass as my sister, if I had one.

One of the doctor's spoke. "Come on Desiree, you've got two little girls who need you."

"Desiree?"

Looking again, I realized that the woman on the table *was* me. No! This couldn't be happening. Running to her side, I began whispering in my own ear. O entered the room, but everything started becoming foggy as I lost my balance and again, got lost in blackness.

~ ODYSSEUS ~

~ CHAPTER 34 ~

"Mr. Kerrigan?" I looked up to her. "Your girls are here. They're ok."

"Des, what about Des?"

"If you'll come with me."

"No, please, God, not Des."

"She's fighting, but it's not looking good."

I walked into the room and saw Des strapped to a table as the doctor sewed her up. Her incision was nothing compared to what I'd seen in battle. The nurse walked me to the head of the table as I stroked her face. She was incredibly pale, too pale.

"We had to give her several units of blood. Unfortunately we had to perform an emergency hysterectomy." Des would be devastated by this.

"The girls?" I held her hand as I pressed my face to the side of hers. "Des." Looking up, "Why isn't she awake?"

"She's had a lot of anesthesia, but we're having trouble getting her to wake up."

I got loud and made my demands, "Where are my girls? She needs her girls. Now!" The doctor nodded as two nurses rushed from the room. "Please wake up, Des." My tears fell on her face as I stroked her face.

The sound of doors and small cries filled the room. Standing, I looked into the cribs as the nurse handed me one of the girls, telling me she was twin A. I sat down with her and pulled her hat back. She had blonde hair and her mother's chin.

"Hello, Ophelia." I got her as close to Des as I could and pleaded with her. "See, you win. You were right, and she looks like an Ophelia." I reached my free arm out as they placed my second daughter in my arms. Dark hair poked out from under her hat as I chuckled, "And she's definitely a Dione. Our own little O and D, our mini-me's. Please, Des. You have to wake up. I can't do this alone."

I heard the faint whisper of someone saying that her heart rate was increasing. Then she began gagging on the breathing tube. They pulled the tube from her mouth as the nurses took the girls from me. Holding her hand, we waited. It took a few minutes, but she opened her eyes. Kissing every inch of her face, I quickly swiped at my snot-covered face as she smiled at me.

"Whas going on?" Her words were slightly slurred, but she was awake.

"Nothing, just rest. Everything's fine."

I woke a few hours later to a hand on my shoulder. Des was in a post-partum room, still sleeping, while I had them keep the girls in the nursery. I slept in the rocking chair, not wanting to leave my wife's side. Heath and Lucy stood in-front of me. I took hold of his arm as he pulled me to my feet. Lucy took my seat, clasping Des' hand, as Heath and I walked into the hall.

I started sobbing as he clapped his arms around me. "I almost lost her."

"But you didn't. The girls?"

He was right, I smiled as I wiped at my tears. "Perfect. They're in the nursery." We both turned when we spotted Lucy.

She closed the distance between us and wrapped her arms around me. "I think she's waking up, O." My eyes got big as she laughed, "Go. We're not going anywhere."

Rushing back into the room, she was moving but her eyes were still closed. When her eyes finally opened, they found mine almost immediately. "Hey, baby." She smiled! "How do you feel?"

"Tired. Sore. What happened?" Her hands drifted to her belly and I saw the panic rise in her eyes knowing she was no longer pregnant.

With tears in my eyes, I reassured her. "The girls are fine. They're perfect."

Choking on her own tears she gasped, "They are?"

"They are. I can have the nurses bring them down. Would you like that?" She nodded. "Ok. I'll be right back."

I sent in Lucy and Heath as I rushed down to the nursery. Flashing my wrist with two pink ID bands around it, I walked over to their cribs. One of the nurses pushed one crib, while I pushed the other down to Des' room.

"I have two little girls eager to meet their Mommy."

Lucy and Heath stood back, awe on their faces as I parked the cribs next to her bed. She was grinning from ear to ear. I picked up little O and walked to the other side of the bed. Placing her in Des' waiting arms, she began looking over every part of her, tears falling down her cheeks. Looking at her band she read it and then pulled the hat from her head.

"She looks like me!"

"Yes, she does." Her tiny hand reached out and grasped onto Des' finger. "You're right. She's definitely an Ophelia."

"Are you sure?"

"Yes." The nurse walked over and handed Des her other daughter and I spotted Heath with a video camera and Lucy snapping pictures. I took Ophelia, while Des looked over Dione. "You're right about her too. Dione."

Des spotted all the dark hair and pulled her hat off. "She's your mini-me."

"What can I say? We make beautiful babies."

"We did good."

"Yes we did." I placed Ophelia in her free arm and squeezed in next to her as Lucy took our picture.

Des looked to Lucy then and asked, "Do you want to hold them?"

"I'd love to, but you just got them. Are you sure?"

Des nodded, "Of course."

Lucy sat down with Dione and Heath with Ophelia as I snapped their picture. "They're so tiny and perfect."

"Listen, we've been meaning to talk to you guys." Lucy and Heath looked up to us, confusion in their eyes. "We'd like you to be their godparents. It'd mean a lot to us."

They smiled at each other and then Heath spoke. "We'd love to, but we need to talk to you guys, too. We're wondering if you'd like to be godparents too?"

"What! Really?" Des was nearly screaming, causing the babies to jump. Lucy nodded her head, tears in her eyes. "When?"

"June."

"June! You've been holding out on me."

Heath interjected. "We wanted to make sure we were well into the second trimester. It's been killing Lucy to not tell you. You're the first people we've told."

"I'm so happy for you." Lucy stood and handed Dione back to her and hugged her. "Do you know what you're having?"

Lucy shook her head. "I took a page from your book, kind of. I don't want to know. I'm just so happy to be having a baby. It just doesn't matter to me if it's a boy or a girl."

"So, it's just one?"

My question had Heath throwing daggers at me as he bit out, "Yes, they checked twice. No twins. Not this time."

"Not this time? Can we please get through this pregnancy before you start mentally impregnating me again?" We laughed at Lucy's comment.

Later that morning the rest of the family made their visit two by two. Mom and Dad were the first to arrive. Bundles of pink balloons, stuffed animals, and flowers now decorated the room. She sat down in the rocking chair, waiting to hold her first set of grandchildren. Placing Dione in one arm and then Ophelia in the other, my mother smiled like I hadn't seen in years.

"What are their names?"

Des looked to me and encouraged me, "Go ahead. You can tell her."

"This here is Dione Marie, twin two, with all the dark hair. Marie is Des' middle name and Dione..."

"Mother of Aphrodite. You carried on my tradition?"

"We did."

"And this little blonde beauty. What's her name?"

I got a little choked up as I said, "This is Ophelia Grace."

"Odysseus?" She looked to Des, who wiped the tears away as my mother realized that Des knew the significance of the name.

"Yes, after my sister and Grace after her grandma."

Des had asked me all those nights ago about D's lost twin, assuming it was a boy. I'd explained to her that D's twin was a girl, and her name was Ophelia. She was my mother's pride and joy and we'd lost her when they were six years old, almost seven. It wasn't until a few weeks later, when the dust had settled that Des asked if we could name one of the girls Ophelia. I wasn't sure it was a good idea, but in the end she was right. We just hoped that D didn't react badly to it.

D seemed fine hearing the news that his niece shared his twin sister's name and everyone loved that we were continuing my mother's tradition. The hardest part of the hospital stay was when I had to tell Des about the hysterectomy. She was heartbroken, but grateful to be alive. It was like she turned a new leaf.

"We have two perfect little girls. I don't need or want anything else." She squeezed my hand and nodded as I added, *"I almost lost you. I don't think I could go through that again."*

"You're right. We're blessed. I love you, O."

We drove home with the twins a few days later. Des' mother shocked us all and came to stay with us for several weeks. It was just what Des needed to get her strength back. Nursing twins, pumping, and trying to heal would have been impossible to do without help. My mother even came and took some night shifts so we could all get some rest.

Months passed and after so much turmoil, we realized life was going to happen to us whether we were ready or not. We were ready. Covered in burp cloths, baby spit, and still wearing yesterday's clothes, I looked around the living room. Des was nursing D as I bottle fed O. She caught me staring at the wonder of motherhood and smiled at me. Bouncers and baby swings littered the floor and I didn't care.

Shortly after, a waddling Lucy and my mother walked in and ordered us to bed. Closing the door, I watched as Des collapsed on the bed.

"I think I'm ok with your mom moving in."

"Bite your tongue woman!"

Mumbling into the pillow she said, "She's a lifesaver. I'd surely be dead if not for her. I love her."

She was already fading as I curled up next to her. "No you wouldn't. We're blessed to have help, but you're a survivor, always have been. We'd be just fine without them, just more sex deprived." She elbowed me in the gut as I laughed.

"Just let me sleep for a few. Then you can have…" She was out.

"I love you, Des. You helped heal my body, then you stole my heart, and the girls and you have completed my soul. Thank you."

Groggily, she startled me with her reply. "You're welcome. Now stop talking so I can sleep. Then you can show me your 'O' face."

THE END...FOR NOW

BODY HEART & SOUL
EVERYTHING DES & O
WERE WILLING TO GIVE.

WHO WILL BE WILL'S
MATCH?

STRENGTH WEAKNESS BOND
BLIND VOWS
VOLUME 3

PLAYLIST

DROWNING BY BANKS
I DON'T WANNA GROW UP BY BEBE
REXHA
YOUNG AND BEAUTIFUL BY LANA DEL
REY
REPLAY BY ZENDAYA
BROKEN ONES BY JACQUIE LEE
LOOK AFTER YOU BY THE FRAY
I'D COME FOR YOU BY NICKELBACK
BREATHE BY RYAN STAR
BEAUTIFUL WITH YOU BY HALESTORM
THIS SUMMER'S GONNA HURT BY
MAROON 5
GOOD FOR YOU BY SELENA GOMEZ
ONLY YOU BY MATTHEW PERRYMAN
JONES
BREATH ME BY SIA
ANGEL BY THEORY OF A DEADMAN
SOUND OF YOUR HEART BY SHAWN
HOOK
THE ONLY REASON BY PUDDLE OF MUDD
NEVER SEEN ANYTHING "QUITE LIKE YOU"
BY THE SCRIPT
CONNECT THE DOTS BY THE SPILL
CANVAS
WAIT BY SARAH MCLACHLAN

MORE FROM J.M. WITT

THE ANCHORED HEARTS SERIES

LETTING GO (VOL. 1) *

HIDING AWAY (VOL. 1.5) *

LETTING GO OF YOU (VOL. 2) *

FADING AWAY (VOL. 2.5) *

LETTING GO OF US (VOL. 3) *

CONCRETE SOUL (VOL. 4) * * * (PAUL'S STORY)

UNTITLED (VOL. 5) * * * (SMITH'S STORY)

DRIFTING AWAY (VOL. 6) * * * (CAL & JANE: WHOLE SERIES EPILOGUE)

THE BLIND VOWS SERIES

VOLUME 1: TRUST, HONOR, LOVE *

VOLUME 2: BODY, HEART, SOUL *

VOLUME 3: STRENGTH, WEAKNESS, BOND * * *

THE CONVICTED SERIES

PUBLISHER: BOOKTROPE

CONVICTED HEART * * *

CONVICTED FIDELITY * * *

CONVICTED JUSTICE * * *

OUT NOW = *   COMING SOON = * * *

ABOUT THE AUTHOR

J.M. RESIDES IN METRO DETROIT, MI WITH HER HUSBAND AND FOUR SMALL CHILDREN.

ALWAYS WANTING TO WRITE ROMANCE NOVELS, SHE FOLLOWED HER DREAMS AFTER HAVING BABY #4, WHO MAY OR MAY NOT BE THE SPAWN OF CHRISTIAN GREY!

SHE HOPES MORE THAN JUST ENJOYING A GOOD BOOK, YOU'LL HAVE AN EXPERIENCE.

YOU CAN FIND HER AT

WWW.JMWITTBOOKS.COM

TWITTER #WITTYMOMAUTHOR

WWW.FACEBOOK.COM/JMWITTBOOKS

AMAZON

www.ingramcontent.com/pod-product-compliance
Lightning Source LLC
Chambersburg PA
CBHW071128200626
46817CB00018B/2454